DEATH
IN THE CHOIR LOFT

RICHARD L. BALDWIN

This novel is a product of the author's imagination. The events described in this story never occurred. Though localities, buildings, and businesses may exist, liberties were taken with their actual location and description. This story has no purpose other than to entertain the reader.

© 2013 Richard L. Baldwin

Published by Buttonwood Press
P.O. Box 716
Haslett, Michigan 48840
www.buttonwoodpress.com

ISBN: 978-0-9823351-9-2
Printed in the United States of America

I dedicate this book to my dear wife, Carol (Patty) Moylan Baldwin. Patty gave me more feedback and input on this book than on any other. Only a small sorority (editor, proofreader, type-setter) are allowed to be critical of my work prior to publication. I usually don't ask Patty to comment because she doesn't enjoy letting me know that something needs attention. With this book, however, I let down my defenses and asked Patty for any help she could provide. She was marvelous, lovingly critical, and kept her yawns to a minimum while listening to my various plots. Near the end of the book's production, she said with a chuckle, "I think you should dedicate this one to me."

No question. Death in the Choir Loft *is dedicated to Patty, with sincere appreciation for all of her loving suggestions.*

OTHER BOOKS BY RICHARD L. BALDWIN

FICTION:

A Lesson Plan for Murder (1998)
ISBN: 0-9660685-0-5. Buttonwood Press.

The Principal Cause of Death (1999)
ISBN: 0-9660685-2-1. Buttonwood Press.

Administration Can Be Murder (2000)
ISBN: 0-9660685-4-8. Buttonwood Press.

Buried Secrets of Bois Blanc: Murder in the Straits of Mackinac (2001)
ISBN: 0-9660685-5-6. Buttonwood Press.

The Marina Murders (2003)
ISBN: 0-9660685-7-2. Buttonwood Press.

A Final Crossing: Murder on the S.S. Badger (2004)
ISBN: 0-9742920-2-8. Buttonwood Press.

Poaching Man and Beast: Murder in the North Woods (2006)
ISBN: 0-9742920-3-6. Buttonwood Press.

The Lighthouse Murders (2007)
ISBN: 978-0-9742920-5-2. Buttonwood Press.

Murder in Thin Air (2008)
ISBN: 978-0-9742920-9-0. Buttonwood Press.

Murder at the Ingham County Fair (2009)
ISBN: 978-0-9823351-0-9. Buttonwood Press.

Murder in Tip-Up Town (2010)
ISBN: 978-0-9823351-2-3. Buttonwood Press.

Assassination at High Speed (2011)
ISBN: 978-0-9823351-4-7. Buttonwood Press.

Murder at the Cherry Festival (2012)
ISBN: 978-0-9823351-6-1. Buttonwood Press.

The Searing Mysteries: Three in One (2001)
ISBN: 0-9660685-6-4. Buttonwood Press.

The Moon Beach Mysteries (2003)
ISBN: 0-9660685-9-9. Buttonwood Press.

The Detective Company (2004; written with Sandie Jones.)
ISBN: 0-9742920-0-1. Buttonwood Press.

SPIRITUAL:

Unity and the Children (2000)
ISBN: 0-9660685-3-X. Buttonwood Press.

NON-FICTION:

The Piano Recital (1999)
ISBN: 0-9660685-1-3. Buttonwood Press.

A Story to Tell: Special Education in Michigan's Upper Peninsula 1902-1975 (1994)
ISBN: 932212-77-8. Lake Superior Press.

Warriors and Special Olympics: The Wertz Warrior Story (2006)
ISBN: 0-9742920-4-4. Buttonwood Press, LLC.

ACKNOWLEDGEMENTS

I thank my editor Anne Ordiway, who works on behalf of my readers by giving them an easy-to-read novel full of interesting characters, twists, and turns in plot lines. Thank you to Joyce Wagner who always picks up the errors in the pre-publication copy. Her eagle eye has saved me time and again. Thank you to Sarah Thomas for once again providing the perfect cover illustration and presenting the text in a readable format. Thank you to the rest of the Buttonwood Press team for their excellent work; Manager Vivian Fahle, Bookkeeper, Jennifer Laing; and CPA, Tom Robinson.

01

Reverend Norris, pastor of the Holy Living Waters Church in Chelsea, Michigan, had called 911 to report a dead person in the choir loft. At 9:06 a.m., a police car, an EMS vehicle and a sheriff's patrol car pulled up to the Holy Living Waters Church in Chelsea, Michigan, arriving quietly with no blaring sirens or flashing lights. The authorities climbed to the loft and found the body of Roland Spencer. The EMS technicians went through routine procedures but found no pulse; the body was cold, the smell of death was becoming stronger, and fluids had begun to drain from the body.

The police treated the choir loft as a crime scene. All door handles and light switches were checked for fingerprints, photos were taken. The body was checked for stab wounds, evidence of strangulation, bullet holes. Nothing was immediately conclusive. The preliminary opinion was that Roland had had a heart attack and died where nobody could see him or hear his cries for help.

The medical examiner arrived and certified death, and the body was transported to the hospital for an autopsy. There was no next of kin to be notified—Roland's parents were both dead, and his brother had died of a heart attack two years before. There wasn't even a best friend. Roland had kept to himself, died alone, and no one needed to be informed of his passing.

♬ ♪ ♬ ♪ ♬

The Holy Living Waters choir director and organist, Isabelle Franklin, was affectionately referred to as "Belle" by the choir members and all of her close friends. Belle was 61 years of age and trim in spite of a long and intense affair with chocolate. Relaxed and out of the public eye, Belle resembled the "school marm" of decades ago: she wore her hair up in a bun, and Ben Franklin-like specs rested near the end of her nose. Belle wore long dresses with tennis shoes. They offered comfort and a better grip, which kept her upright and mobile.

When the occasion demanded it, however, Belle dressed in fashionable attire, letting her hair down to reveal flowing dark brown tresses. She easily could have passed for a Wall Street executive. Her "dress" glasses were stylish, and her makeup took ten years off her age.

Belle's phone rang shortly after ten o'clock while she cleaned up the breakfast dishes. She noted from caller ID that it was Reverend Norris. "Belle, I've some bad news."

"Something's happened to Roland?" Belle asked, sensing the news would relate to Roland Spencer.

"He's dead, Belle. Winston found him this morning in the choir loft."

There was a pause while Belle took in what she had just heard. Almost instantly, she recalled the light going off in the church before she entered the back door. "Where is the body now?"

"The body has been taken to the hospital for an autopsy."

"Last evening I saw Roland's car in the parking lot. I looked for him, thinking maybe he fell and couldn't get up, or maybe he had a stroke. I looked in the choir loft, but didn't see him."

"He was wedged between the pews."

"Oh my, I can't believe it."

"The police will want to talk to you, Belle."

"Why?"

"You and other choir members were the last to see him, and it appears he died after choir practice."

"Oh, I see. Okay. Do I contact the police or will they call me?" Belle asked.

"They'll contact you."

"The choir will be devastated."

"Will you join me in prayer, Belle?" asked the Reverend.

"Surely."

"Father, we thank you for Roland and the gifts he brought to our congregation. We trust and believe he is now singing in Heaven. Please bring peace to all who loved him and who will be grieving his passing. Amen."

Belle added, "Amen."

♬ ♪ ♬ ♪ ♬

The news of Roland's death spread throughout Chelsea like a grass fire. Reverend Norris decided to let people who were coming to the scene enter the church and sit quietly in the pews. The police had only cordoned off the choir room and loft. Every fifteen minutes or so, Reverend Norris would appear and lead a short prayer followed by The Lord's Prayer.

Members and others came to the church to pray or simply think of Roland and the unexplainable way he died, right in Christ's home on earth.

A television crew arrived and interviewed Reverend Norris, the front of the church serving as a backdrop. A tall gentleman with a full head of grey hair, Reverend Norris carried himself with great dignity. He was respected in the community, sat on numerous boards, and was the leader of ecumenism in Chelsea.

Reverend Norris was a family man. He was proud of his family. They often accompanied him to a variety of social events or joined him for dinner. He was never without his "favorite" son or daughter as he liked to call them.

The reporter continued, "The melodious tones of Roland Spencer have been silenced. Roland died in the choir loft of Holy Living Waters Church, the building behind me. He was at the church practicing for an upcoming choir performance of the Messiah. An autopsy is scheduled for later today. We will bring you additional information as it becomes available."

Belle called the choir's phone tree. Alerting Phyllis, the first name on the tree, she started the network that let everyone know of the death of their peer.

The police went into Roland's home and discovered Aria, Roland's dog, alone and hungry. They called the county animal control office, who sent an officer to pick up the orphaned dog. The officers then made sure the home was safe for locking, and they'd patrol throughout the day in case the announcement of Roland's death might entice looters to drive by and look for opportunities to break in.

Oddly enough, a steady stream of people visited the church throughout the day. Belle and Reverend Norris had no idea that Roland had touched so many lives. As has become common practice, people left a flower or a bouquet at the door of the church, along with votive candles and notes of love.

♫ ♪ ♫ ♪ ♫

Belle was happily married to Henry "Hank" Franklin who had served 30 years as a school band director and following retirement had become an assistant to the high school band director. Every day, Hank wore blue jeans, a dress shirt, and running shoes, but never a tie. He was a gifted bridge player. In fact, he and Belle were masters and in their spare time, they'd travel to bridge tournaments throughout the midwest.

Belle and Hank chose toasted cheese sandwiches and tomato soup for dinner because neither was hungry after the tragedy that had visited Chelsea. After Hank offered grace, Belle cooled her soup and quietly said, "This is not good for me. I'm afraid of a witch hunt."

"Witch hunt? What do you mean?" Hank asked, surprised at Belle's comment.

"I mean I may be the community scapegoat for this."

"A heart attack or a stroke—how could you be a cause for either?" Hank asked.

"He didn't die of natural causes," Belle said.

"Oh, I am sure he did," Hank replied. "Are you thinking he was murdered?"

"Yes. I'm certain of it."

"Why, Belle? Did you see or hear something?"

"My intuition. It's been building to this."

"What has been building to this?" Hank asked, seeking some clarification from his wife.

"Roland. He's been acting strange."

"So, you don't really know how he died. You just think he was murdered, right?"

Belle had yet to sip her soup or take a bite of her sandwich. "All I'm saying is if this is not explained, I will be in everyone's mind as the killer."

"Eat your dinner, Belle," Hank urged. "It will be explained, and you won't be seen as a murderer. Trust me!"

"I'd better get to the church. The choir is meeting there at seven. Are you coming with me?"

"If you don't mind, sure."

"Fine with me," Belle replied, walking toward the sink with her dishes. "I'll clean up the dishes when we get home."

"I'll pick up, it will only take a minute," Hank said, reaching for the scrub brush. "I wish you would have eaten some dinner. You need something in your stomach. This is an emotional time for all of us."

Belle didn't acknowledge Hank. She retired quietly to their bathroom to freshen up before driving to church.

When they arrived, Belle greeted the choir members, giving each a hug and sharing a tear with many. Belle suggested they face the choir loft and sing one of their favorite hymns. With a tear falling onto her cheek, she led the choir in a solemn version of "How Great Thou Art". It was an emotional moment for the choir and for those who had come to church to mourn.

02

The drama had begun the previous evening when the choir had finished rehearsing Handel's Messiah, which was to be performed in the high school auditorium in a couple of weeks. People came from miles around to hear this concert, which was an Easter tradition in the small town of Chelsea. The townsfolk knew to arrive early because by concert time, not a seat was to be had. In fact, some ticket holders even brought lawn chairs in case they arrived to find a packed auditorium.

The rehearsal had been exhausting because the music was so intense and the singing of the "Hallelujah Chorus" demanded considerable effort. The piece was full of emotion and energy, which perhaps was why Roland Spencer paused to catch his breath shortly after the last "hallelujah". Roland didn't walk out with the others to the choir room. He stayed behind to sit down, breathe deeply, and to gather his music.

Roland Spencer was huge, to put it mildly, but he was always smartly-dressed. His shoes were meticulously shined, and his handlebar moustache was neatly trimmed and perfectly twirled. Roland was also a perfect bass singer resembling the late tenor Pavarotti. Members of the congregation often said they felt chills when Roland sang a solo or performed a segment of a piece. The entire church often reverberated as his low tones echoed melodiously over the sanctuary.

Roland, a bachelor, lived with his pug dog, Aria. She was named Aria because she would lift her chin and howl for minutes at a time whenever she heard Roland's CD of Maria Callas. Roland's only female relationship had been with a high school girl who told him at the last minute she didn't want to go to the senior prom with him. That rejection struck deep into Roland, like a pick plunging into an ice block. If she had known how devastated Roland would be, she might not have called off the date. In fact, the girl expected Roland to be relieved, but that rejection caused his mistrust of relationships. His singing became enough for him. Everyone loved him for his singing, and that satisfied him.

Roland had befriended Dick Fox, a 24 year-old neighbor with a disability, and hired him to walk Aria a couple of times a day, feed her, and for all intents and purposes, be her caregiver. Roland agreed to pay Dick fifty dollars a week for his services. The arrangement seemed fair to both Dick and the director of the Arthur Hills Group Home, Megan Morgan, but Roland sometimes went months without paying his promised fee. When he did pay, it was only for one week, with no mention of back pay. Dick's disability was such that he didn't realize he was being taken advantage of, but Megan did because some of Dick's care depended on the money for his expenses.

Roland dismissed repeated attempts to collect, and with each passing week without remuneration, Megan would boil in anger, envisioning some way to make Roland suffer for not paying his agreed-upon fee.

Megan was 36 years old. She had been the director of the Arthur Hills Group Home for the past eleven years. She was a domineering woman. She set the standards and made sure that clients adhered to them. She had not married and had her own room at the group home. She was petite with short hair and bangs. She was smartly dressed and wore two watches, one on each wrist. No one knew why and she didn't choose to explain it to anyone.

♫ ♪ ♫ ♪ ♫

Following choir rehearsal the night before, Belle had set out for the grocery store. As she approached her car, she had noticed Roland's vehicle still in the church lot. *That's odd*, she thought. She could think of no logical reason for Roland to still be in the church; the building was dark and locked. Nor would he have left with another choir member. The only thing she could think of was that the car's battery was dead or it had a mechanical problem.

Belle continued to the store, purchased the items on her list, and headed home. She went a bit out of her way to pass the church; Roland's car was still there. Belle had a key to the church because of evening choir rehearsals. She pulled in to the lot, parked, and walked toward the back door as a full moon cast shadows on the church's towering steeple.

As she approached the back door, Belle saw a light go out in the church. She walked around to the front, hoping to see Roland leaving. She saw no sign of him, but noted a woman walking a dog down the street. Nothing seemed out of the ordinary, so she returned to the back door. Belle had no fear of entering. From all she could tell, the lights were off and no one should be inside. But Roland could have fainted, fallen and couldn't get up, or after his breathing difficulty there was a remote chance that he might be, Heaven forbid, dead.

Belle opened the door and reached for the light switch beside the door panel. She flipped it up, slowly entered, and began calling, "Roland? Roland?" She made her way to the choir room, unlocked the door, and turned on the light. No one was there. She opened the door to the choir loft and glanced inside. Moonlight shone through the stained-glass windows, casting a shadow of Christ onto the altar. The shadowy scene caused Belle to think, *Oh my, God is surely present in all of this beauty.*

Belle heard nothing. And, after a quick look around, she concluded that Roland was not in the loft, the choir room, or the church. Her fear that something had happened to him appeared unfounded. After turning off lights and locking doors, she returned to her car.

Sitting behind the wheel, Belle entered Roland's number on her cell phone, but there was no answer. She called a couple of choir members to ask if they knew his whereabouts, but they didn't. She called the Chelsea Grill where Roland usually ate dinner, but he had not been in. She called the local hospital, but he had not been admitted. Finally, she called the police to ask about his whereabouts. They had no report on him.

Roland had disappeared off the face of the earth. He had to be somewhere, perhaps with someone, and no doubt he was safe and secure. Belle knew he was a movie buff, and the theater was within walking distance of the church. She called the theater and spoke to the manager who said, "I didn't see him this evening. I'll walk up and down the aisles and call you if I can find him." He didn't call her back.

03

APRIL 20 • CHELSEA, MICHIGAN

Preliminary autopsy results ruled Roland's manner of death as inconclusive and his cause of death unknown. The toxicology report would take days or weeks to complete. In this case, the analysis of body fluids would be vital; what was in his blood when he died would probably indicate the cause of death.

♫ ♪ ♫ ♪ ♫

Chelsea area choir directors and organists met at The Chelsea Café to plan the Messiah. After everyone had settled, Reverend Bellamy of the Baptist church spoke up. "I move we cancel the concert this year."

"I second that," responded Judy Zack, the organist of the First Presbyterian church.

"Discussion," Reverend Bellamy said. Several hands went up around the U-shaped private meeting area.

Ester Dalrympal of Our Lady of Sorrows said, "Absolutely not! This is a tradition in Chelsea. People expect this concert, and the money raised helps us provide concert-goers with better and better productions. I will vote NO, and I encourage all of you to do the same." Light applause followed.

Next to speak was Reverend Bellamy. "I made the motion because I believe people's minds will be on the missing Roland Spencer and not Handel's masterpiece. Every eye in the place will be focused on the spot where Roland stood for years. If we don't cancel, the concert will be all about Roland, and not the lyrics and our voices."

"You're saying this concert would be all about a dead Roland?" the organist from The First Methodist church said, speaking before being recognized. "You don't think concert-goers will be caught up in the masterpiece? Give the listeners some credit, Reverend! Those who knew Roland will note his absence, but I think the audience will quickly bring their attention to the piece."

Reverend Bellamy recognized Pastor Ingersoll of the First Church of the Nazarene. "I suggest that we go ahead with the concert, but offer a moment of silence and a prayer in Roland's honor. We can offer a tribute, and afterward we can focus on our rendition of the classic."

"I like that!" Belle exclaimed. Most of the heads nodded.

"Then I withdraw my motion," Reverend Bellamy said to a roomful of smiles.

"And, I withdraw my second," Judy Zack added.

The concert would go ahead as planned.

♫ ♪ ♫ ♪ ♫

Belle received a call from the county animal control office.

"Mrs. Franklin?"

"Yes."

"This is the Animal Control Office in Ann Arbor. You may know Mrs. Lopez. She is the president of Friends of the Humane Society."

"Yes, I know Tricia."

"We have Mr. Spencer's dog here. She is extremely agitated, confused, almost having a dog's version of a nervous breakdown. Tricia thought you might be a good dog-sitter until a permanent home can be found. Might you and your husband agree to such an arrangement?"

"I suppose we could do that. The dog is a cute little pug, as I recall."

"That's right. The name on her tag is 'Aria'."

"Shall I come over to the humane society to pick up Aria? Is there paperwork?"

"Everything will be taken care of. Yes, just stop in and we'll handle the rest. And, thank you very much, Mrs. Franklin."

♫ ♪ ♫ ♪ ♫

Belle needed to talk with Reverend Norris. He welcomed Belle into his office. "You wanted to see me?" he asked.

"Yes. I felt that we should sort of clear the air."

"Clear the air of what?" Reverend asked, sensing tension in Belle's manner.

"The police told me they were interviewing me because you told them I had a confrontation with Roland, raising suspicion that I may have killed him."

"I'm sorry. I was simply answering the officer's question."

"What question was that?" Belle asked.

"He wanted to know if Roland had had any confrontations with anyone recently. Roland had stopped me in the hall one day and mentioned that he didn't appreciate your continuous nagging, and if it kept up, he might drop out of the choir."

"That's interesting. My 'continuous nagging' is called 'choir directing'. A group of voices needs direction, and that's exactly what I do. Our choir is good because we practice until I am confident we can present the music as the composer intended. The interactions I have with the choir are not confrontations, and they can't be characterized as 'continuous nagging' no matter what Roland said."

"I stand corrected," Reverend Norris stated. "In retrospect, I probably should not have considered it a 'confrontation'."

"Thank you. Now, I have a confession of sorts," Belle said solemnly. "I told the officer who interviewed me that you had a confrontation with Roland."

"When he didn't show up for the charity concert, I assume?"

"Yes. Ironically, Roland mentioned to me one day that he feared your anger."

"I can understand that," Reverend Norris replied. "I was pretty upset, to put it mildly."

"It also sounds like Roland was playing us off one another," Belle concluded.

"It appears that's what happened, yes."

"So, I'm sorry I gave the impression you could be a suspect," Belle said, looking Reverend Norris in the eye. "I spoke because I was upset that you made me look guilty."

"Apology accepted. And I apologize as well. Are we back in each other's good graces?" Reverend Norris asked.

"I feel better. Thanks."

"Amen."

♫ ♪ ♫ ♪ ♫

That evening, Belle and Hank talked at the dinner table. Belle began, "You do realize that I am 'suspect number one'?" Belle asked.

"I see why you think so, but I don't agree."

"I think I need to become an investigator, if only to save my own reputation."

"You would be great, Belle. You're intuitive, you problem-solve. I would be your number-one fan."

"Thanks. You know how much I admire Lou Searing…"

"Maybe he could give you some tips," Hank interrupted, before Belle could finish her thought.

"That's exactly what I was thinking. I'll try to contact him. He's busy, which means he's probably impossible to reach."

"Can't hurt to try," Hank said.

Belle admired Lou, a private investigator from Grand Haven. Belle had read and enjoyed all of his books written under the pen name Richard L. Baldwin. She liked the way Lou and Jack Kelly worked together to solve difficult cases. She knew that if she didn't solve Roland's death, she would be forever suspect. She certainly didn't want to carry that stigma around the rest of her life.

To Belle's surprise, Lou answered the phone after just a few rings. Belle introduced herself.

"I am happy to speak with you, Mr. Searing. I've enjoyed all of your books, and I admire your investigative skills."

"Thank you, but you didn't call to sing my praises. Can I help?" Lou asked.

"I live in Chelsea, and I'm between a rock and a hard place."

"Let's see if we can resolve your dilemma, then. Give me some basic information, please," Lou said.

"I'm a church organist and choir director. A member of the choir died in the choir loft a couple of days ago."

"Was he murdered?" Lou asked, interrupting Belle's telling of the situation.

"I don't know. The autopsy was inconclusive, so, if he was murdered, it wasn't obvious. You know, like a gunshot, stabbing, being clobbered over the head, or strangled. I suppose he could have been poisoned."

"OK, go on."

"I may have been the last to see him. That evening I saw his car in the church parking lot, which was odd. So, I went into the church thinking he might have fallen—he was a huge man. I also thought he might have had a stroke. Anyway, I looked in the choir loft but didn't see him because apparently he lay between the pews. My fingerprints were found on some of the door knobs, of course. Since I went back into the church, people find me an easy target, thinking I must have killed him."

"So, the medical examiner didn't certify death as natural, meaning heart attack, stroke or the like?" Lou asked.

"Not yet. I guess they're waiting for blood tests."

"Well, they may conclude he died a natural death," Lou surmised. "If he didn't, the autopsy should report how he died. If murder is feasible, we can investigate. Did he have any known enemies? How about skeletons in his closet?" Lou asked.

"Well, we never really know another person," Belle began. "Roland seemed to be a loner who lived a pretty simple life. From what I saw, his daily routine wouldn't suggest any cause for someone to murder him."

"No one has put forth a theory since he died?" Lou asked.

"I think Roland would suspect Phyllis, another member of the choir. She brings peanuts to choir practice. Everyone knows Roland asked her to leave them in her car or home because he was severely allergic, but she brings them anyway."

"That's interesting. So they had little love for one another?" Lou asked.

"Two very different people with different agendas," Belle replied. "Phyllis is quiet, unassuming, but not one to leave her peanuts behind because of Roland's allergy. She didn't eat them during practice, nor did she pass them around or offer Roland one. At least not that I saw."

"We'll put Phyllis on the suspect list for now," Lou said. "Anything else?"

"You know, I just called to ask if you would be willing to meet me and give me a few pointers in investigating this mess. It sounds like you're jumping right in, as if you plan to help me solve it."

"Of course, why not? I love to work on a mystery," Lou admitted. "Some people like crossword puzzles, or gardening. I like a problem to solve, and you certainly have one, especially if the toxicology report indicates possible murder."

"Well, thank you, Mr. Searing! You're wonderful. But don't you think you should check with Mrs. Searing before taking this on?"

"Carol will be fine with it. The last case was number thirteen, and I'm still upright and mobile. Besides, this doesn't sound like a shoot'em-up mystery, if it was a murder, which I frankly doubt. But, we can treat it as such and be proactive."

"What's my next step?" Belle asked.

"I'd like to meet you, look around, talk to people, and we can go from there. In the meantime, if authorities decide it was a natural death, let me know, okay?"

"Thank you. I'll give you my number and you can call whenever a visit is possible," Belle said, and dictated her phone number. "You may wish to come on the evening of a choir rehearsal, if you want to talk to the other members."

"That's a good idea. I'll also want to talk to your police chief since I'd be in his jurisdiction. I want it clear that I'm not trying to upstage or interfere with his work."

"I can arrange a meeting when you come down."

"Fine. I'll check my calendar and be back with you soon."

"Thank you so much, Mr. Searing."

"My name is Lou. There's no need to be formal. Oh, and by the way, don't jump right into being Jessica Fletcher. We'll need to talk to the police chief so you know the ground rules of trying to investigate something as a citizen."

"OK, thank you, Lou. I'm looking forward to meeting you in person."

"Talk with you soon."

♫ ♪ ♫ ♪ ♫

Belle had no sooner hung up when there was a knock on her door. She wasn't expecting anyone, but maybe the Girl Scouts were out in full force with their cookies. She went to the front door, looked out a side window and saw a police officer. She thought, *I hope another choir member hasn't died.*

Belle opened the door and prepared for some bad news. "Mrs. Franklin?"

"Yes."

"I need you to come with me," the officer said.

"Why?"

"I've been told to pick you up. Our detective wants to talk with you."

"Do I need to call my lawyer?" Belle asked.

"Might be a good idea," the officer remarked.

Belle took out her cell phone and called Dennis Intrieri. A receptionist answered, "Intrieri and Starkey. How may I direct your call?"

"I'd like to speak to Dennis, please."

"He's not in. I can give you his voice mail."

"Please do." After the introductory spiel, Belle said, "Dennis, it's Belle Franklin. A police officer is at the house taking me to the station, I don't know why. Please call me on my cell. You have the number, I'm sure. I will not say a word till I hear from you. Thank you."

Belle turned to the officer, "Are we in a big hurry? Can I feed Roland's dog before we go?"

"Please hurry."

Being told to hurry only encouraged Belle to take her time, which she did. After feeding Aria, she picked up her purse and a light jacket, locked her front door, and went with the officer to the squad car. She noticed several neighbors on either side watching the proceedings. *Oh my, Lord have mercy*, she said to herself.

As the car pulled out of the drive, Belle's cell phone rang. It was Dennis. "What's the problem, Belle?"

"Not sure. I'm on the way to the station."

"I'll call Chief Purdy and find out what's going on," Dennis said. "If I call you back, I'll have advice for you. If I don't call back, cooperate."

"Will do. Thanks, Dennis."

♬ ♪ ♬ ♪ ♬

Once at the station, Belle was asked to view hundreds of photos. There had been a mysterious death at a church in Illinois.

The police had several photos of suspects in the Illinois murder, and the Chelsea Police wanted to be sure that Belle had not seen anyone in the photos in or around the church, or even in town.

"Why do I need a police escort to look at mug shots?" Belle asked, perturbed. "You can't begin to imagine the gossip going through my neighborhood. As far as my neighbors are concerned, I must be a hardened criminal."

"You have an unlisted number, and we don't know your cell phone number. Neither Reverend Norris nor the church receptionist was in, so I directed an officer to escort you in, to save you some gas money."

"How thoughtful. You could have explained. You should have cuffed me for dramatic effect," Belle said sarcastically.

"I guess we didn't take into account nosy neighbors. Sorry."

"Whatever. I know the neighborhood gossip leader. I'll just explain why I'm here. In about fifteen minutes the word will spread, and hopefully I'll be exonerated."

Belle maintained that she had not seen any of the men in the photos. The police thanked her and, following apologies, drove her home in an unmarked car.

♫ ♪ ♫ ♪ ♫

Belle called Phyllis and graciously invited herself to a private conversation.

"Isn't it terrible—Roland dying and right there in the choir loft?" Belle began on a solemn note.

"Yes," Phyllis agreed. "We all have to go sooner or later, and not only do we not get to choose when, but we also often can't choose where."

"I am a suspect because my fingerprints are on the church doorknobs, and I came back to the church that evening," Belle admitted. "I'm trying to solve Roland's death to clear my name."

"You would never harm anyone, Belle. I can vouch for you."

"Thanks. Many could, I guess. I just have to let time heal, and it will."

"Why did you call?" Phyllis asked.

"I was wondering… did you know that Roland was allergic to peanuts?" Belle asked.

"Oh, no, not this peanut thing again. Peanuts are my favorite snack. I have brought peanuts in my purse to choir practice for years, and he never so much as sneezed. I'm absolutely convinced that Roland wasn't allergic to them. You knew Roland—he'd find the simplest thing to get upset about."

"I've noticed that, too."

"My doctor told me to be safe, never to take the peanuts out of the bag which is tightly-sealed, and never take the bag out of my purse. So, I haven't."

"Good. But when the EMS crew removed the body, they reported finding shells and broken peanuts on the floor nearby. Did you share peanuts with Roland after choir practice?"

"Absolutely not, Belle! Do you think I'm insane? Why would I ever do that?"

"I'm just telling you what the police know. I wondered whether you had given him some peanuts, that's all."

"I certainly did not," Phyllis replied. "I tolerated Roland but I can't imagine talking with him, let alone giving him peanuts!"

"I had to ask."

"I'm glad you did, so I can set the record straight."

"What do you think happened to Roland?" Belle asked.

"To be honest, my money's on suicide."

"Suicide?"

"Think about it," Phyllis reasoned. "Roland was depressed, lonely, in ill health, hung around with a mutt, and had only a bass voice to bring him any attention."

"Hmm, I never thought of suicide. But in the choir loft?" Belle asked.

"Can you think of a better place, and after singing 'The Halleluiah Chorus,' no less?"

"How would he have killed himself?"

"Brought his own peanuts."

"Possible."

"And, he could torment me in the process."

"It's a possibility, Phyllis. Thanks for talking with me."

"You're welcome," replied Phyllis. "One more thought. Remember when you asked each choir member to give you a list of favorite hymns? As I recall, you were going to choose a dozen for us to perform at a community concert."

"Yes, I remember, but I never did anything with it. I simply put it on the back burner. Why do you bring it up?" Belle asked.

"Believe me, I am no detective, but I thought that there may be a clue in Roland's list."

"Interesting, Phyllis. I have those lists in a file in the choir room. I'll find Roland's and see if anything jumps out at me."

"Good luck, Belle."

04

It was the most beautiful spring day the citizens of Chelsea remembered in recent years. Flowers of every kind offered bright colors and soft fragrances. A row of lilac trees next to the church had exploded in purple and the aroma wafted into the sanctuary. The police had removed the yellow caution tape, indicating their investigation was complete.

So, with a blue sky and the earth decked in spring finery, the funeral for Roland Spencer was about to begin. There was no casket; Roland's will had specified that he would be cremated. At the front of the church a stand held Roland's urn. A large framed photograph of a smiling Roland sat to the right of the urn and sprays of flowers surrounded the frame.

Reverend Norris officiated. The choir, in their blue robes, were seated in the loft. There was a display of flowers where Roland had sung week after week for years. Ushers had asked a number of people to scoot closer to the middle of the pews in order to accommodate more visitors. While the opening prayer was said and the choir sang "Holy, Holy, Holy," the ushers were setting up additional seats in the narthex, hoping that the fire chief didn't plan to attend.

If it is possible to have a funeral where everything went as planned, it was Roland's. Those in attendance thought that Reverend Norris's remarks were appreciative of Roland and the choir did a remarkable job, given the grief most felt. After the service, the choir sold hundreds of CD. Roland had designated the church as beneficiary of the money collected from the sale of the CD as a memorial when he died.

On Monday morning, April 24, a revised autopsy report was made available to law enforcement and, hence, the media. The cause of death was listed as anaphylaxis, an allergic reaction to allergens. Belle asked to review the on-the-scene EMS reports, which indicated that peanut shells, peanut fragments, and some intact nuts were found near the body. The question was obvious: where had the nuts come from? *Roland wouldn't have been able to see them when he took his place in the loft,* Belle thought; if the cause of death was anaphylaxis, the person who scattered the peanuts around that area of the loft was guilty of murder.

In that respect, there was only one current suspect: Phyllis.

Lou Searing, 71 years young, bald, wearing glasses and two hearing aids, arrived in Chelsea on Tuesday, April 25, meeting Belle at the Holy Living Waters Church at 1:00 p.m. The choir would practice that evening, and Lou would drive back to Grand Haven following his interviews with some members.

After greeting each other with smiles and handshakes, Lou said, "Let's get down to business. I called the chief of police to work with you in determining how Roland and those peanuts came to occupy the same area in the choir loft. The chief agreed to share the information they've collected, and in return, I will do the same."

"That's great," Belle replied.

"Chief Purdy said they're working on the Spencer case, but it has low priority because he considers it a natural death until new evidence suggests murder. He did confirm that, if it is murder, Roland's choir mates are suspects, if only because they were the last to see him."

"I understand," Belle said.

"But, he didn't seem to mind you investigating. You can't claim to be working on behalf of any law enforcement unit, but you know that. He didn't think he needed to talk with you, given that I can tell you what you can and can't do."

"And he welcomed you becoming involved?" Belle asked.

"I wouldn't say 'welcomed', but he said he respected me, and he had no problem with my working on the case."

"I asked you to help me solve it, but not to solve it for me," Belle demurred.

"I know, and that's why I'll give you leads to follow, then let you proceed, checking often to see if you found the right road."

"That's acceptable. I am humbled by your confidence in me. What do I do first?" Belle asked.

"You interviewed Phyllis—great beginning. She is suspect, and you reached out to her. By the way, you need a notebook, iPad—something to record notes, including who you talked with, when, and what you learned. You also need some business cards to leave with people, for they sometimes recall something they should have told you."

"What do I put on the cards?" Belle asked, puzzled.

"Simple contact information; e-mail, cell phone number."

"Why is that?"

"Convenience for them and privacy for you."

"I didn't think we had privacy any longer in this country?" Belle asked sarcastically.

"In reality, I suppose we don't. It doesn't matter what number you use, they just need a way to reach you."

"Do I put on the card that I am a church choir director and organist, or something that legitimizes my asking questions about a murder?"

"Let's be creative. How about, 'Organist by Day, Sleuth by Night'. It has a nice ring to it, right?" Lou asked smugly.

"I like that!" Belle replied with a grin. "I'll get the cards made up right away. Thanks, Lou."

♫ ♪ ♫ ♪ ♫

That afternoon Lou and Belle took time to chart out on paper what they knew. In the 'suspects' column, they put down Phyllis and Belle. Under the 'people to interview' column were the people Roland saw regularly: neighbors, choir members, grocery store workers and the theater manager.

Belle suggested a column titled 'Peanuts' since that seemed to be the cause of death. Lou added, "We need to add an 'experts' column, for people like a pathologist, an allergist, a forensic specialist, and the medical examiner."

Finally Lou went over protocol seriously. "You can't claim to represent any law enforcement unit. You can't carry a gun. You need to know what you can ask and what you can't; if you know a lawyer, you might want to speak with him or her about this. If you do or say the wrong thing, it could come up in court and cause a dismissal of the case."

"That's a good idea. I can talk with my attorney, Dennis Intrieri," Belle replied. "He is the town's well-known attorney, and it was difficult to break into his list of clients. I'm one of the lucky ones."

"Okay, if he can give you a little time, that'd be great."

"Before you leave, Lou, I want to share something with you. Several weeks ago I asked each member of the choir to make a list of their favorite hymns. My plan was to choose the most popular for our community concert. I know that Roland submitted a list, and Phyllis suggested that I look at the lists his list to see if a pattern popped up."

"Did a clue surface?" Lou asked.

"No, but that doesn't mean a clue isn't there."

"What were his hymns?"

Belle handed Lou the list and Lou read the hymns as Roland had written them. "They are common hymns. 'Just a Closer Walk with Thee', 'The Old Rugged Cross', 'Ashes'. Nothing seems obvious. I don't see any pattern."

"I'll study the list, because it might indicate what was on Roland's mind. It might give us something we need to break the case."

"Good idea."

♫ ♪ ♫ ♪ ♫

Lou arrived at Holy Living Waters Church a few minutes before 7 p.m. As he walked in, he heard the choir going through warm-up exercises. He followed the voices to the choir loft and saw Belle at the organ giving directions. She motioned for Lou to join her on the organ bench.

"Your attention, please," Belle said with authority. The voices ceased, and the members looked at Belle and Lou.

"This is my friend, Lou Searing," Belle began. "He has solved about a dozen murders in Michigan. I've asked him to help us learn how Roland died. As you know, I'm a suspect, but I didn't kill him. Roland died of anaphylaxis, according to the autopsy report. We all know that Phyllis carries peanuts with her; I've talked with her, and I'm confident she did not expose Roland to them at any time. Lou, this is a wonderful choir, and I am privileged to work with them every week."

"Thank you, Belle. I love music and choirs. I myself can't carry a tune in a handbag, as my father used to say, but my mother was an accomplished musician and provided countless hours of enjoyment playing the piano. So I respect and admire what you do.

"We're not sure that this was a murder," Lou continued. "Roland's death could be natural, and I shan't be surprised if that's the final determination. Or, it could have been an accident. However, if the authorities determine he was murdered, then I will assist Belle as she investigates. The one thing we know is that Roland was at choir rehearsal the night he died, but, we don't think that Roland returned to the choir room after rehearsal, but that he stayed here in the loft. Is that true?"

Everyone either nodded or said, "Yes."

"And I assume none of you saw Roland after practice—in the parking lot or elsewhere in the church. Is that also true?"

Again, nods and "yeses" were the norm.

"Now, did anyone see Roland the day of rehearsal, or even a couple of days before? And if you did, did he say anything about not feeling well?"

A hand shot up in the tenor section. Lou acknowledged the woman.

"I talked to Roland in the choir room before practice. I told him he always looked dapper. I was just in a mood to give him a compliment."

"And, he said..." Belle led.

"He just said, 'Thanks'. But, then he took his music folder and threw it on the floor."

"I remember that," Tom Everlast, a baritone, said. "I was beside him and I asked, 'Everything okay'?"

"He couldn't bend over to retrieve it, so I picked it up," Tom explained. "Now that I think about it, some of the music came out, as well as some other papers. I noticed a doctor's prescription, but I didn't think anything of it. I just put the music and papers back in the folder, lifted it, and handed it to Roland."

"You didn't see what the prescription was for?" Lou asked.

"Are you kidding me?" Tom replied. "I can't read what the doctor writes on my prescriptions, let alone another's."

After a ripple of laughter, Lou continued, "Did anyone notice Roland acting strangely during rehearsal?" There was no response.

"If anyone has a theory about what happened that night you can say so now. Or, if you'd rather tell Belle privately, talk to her after rehearsal."

"I personally think Roland just gave up," Bill Harrison said. "The reason he threw down his music folder was because our new music in it was what he sang at his brother's funeral, and he hardly got through that. Maybe depression just took over and he couldn't handle the stress any longer."

"Thank you, Bill," Belle said.

"Could you elaborate, please?" Lou asked.

"I think his blood pressure got too high, and the adrenaline racing through his system just caused him to collapse," Bill explained. "Mind you, I'm no doctor, but think about it: overweight, no friends, almost always in conflict with someone, always angry about something—doesn't that add up to pressure that might cause death? He sort of killed himself, a crazy form of suicide is probably what I'm suggesting."

"Thank you, Bill," Lou replied. "Any other thoughts?" There were none.

"Good," Lou concluded. "If you don't mind, I'd love to hear you sing and then I'll slip out. I am confident that Roland's death will be explained."

♫ ♪ ♫ ♪ ♫

The next day, Wednesday, April 26th, Belle spoke with Winston Saturn, the church custodian who had found Roland's body in the loft. The two sipped coffee in the Fellowship Hall.

"Finding Roland must have been quite upsetting for you," Belle remarked to get the conversation rolling.

"Yeah, it was. I've never seen a dead person before. I mean, in a casket, yes, but not just laid out like he was."

"What did you do when you found him?" Belle asked.

"Well, I didn't know he was dead. I thought maybe he had fainted and couldn't get up. I knelt down beside him and checked for a pulse, but there wasn't one. His heart wasn't beating. I went to Reverend Norris and told him, and he took it from there."

"Did you see any peanuts or peanut shells around his body?" Belle asked.

"Yes, and I can probably explain that. I had some peanuts in my bib overalls, and when I stooped over to listen to his heart, they probably fell out. I didn't take the time to pick them up—just took off to find Reverend Norris."

"So the peanuts were yours?" Belle asked, surprised.

"Probably. I keep a big bag of them in my quarters. I take some out to the birds, and I keep some for myself. I don't want to leave a mess, so I put the cracked shells in my bib overalls. When I get home, I clean the bib out. Nuts are good for you, you know, and our birds love the treat. It keeps them coming back."

"Are you sure the peanuts fell out when you checked for a heartbeat? They didn't fall out a day earlier around where you found Roland?"

"No, they would have fallen out while I was listening for a heartbeat. No question about it."

"Have you any idea how Roland died?" Belle asked.

"He was a big man. Heart attack is all I can imagine."

"Thank you, Winston. If you have any other ideas about this, don't hesitate to call me or leave a note in my mailbox in the church office."

"Yes, ma'am. Now, please excuse me, I have to put posters up about the church craft show this weekend."

"Sure. We'll talk again, I'm sure," Belle said, ending the conversation. She rose, then hesitated. "Oh wait, I have just one more question."

"Okay."

"I was straightening up the choir room, and I noticed that Roland's music folder was gone."

"I threw it in the recycling bin," Winston admitted.

"You did? Why?" Belle asked, surprised.

"Well, what good is a music folder if the person it belonged to is dead?"

"I see your reasoning, but I wish you hadn't done that."

"I put it in the recycling bin, and the recycle truck doesn't come for a few more days. Do you want me to dig around and find it for you?"

"Yes, please. I hate to have you take the time to paw through reams of papers, but it would help me."

"Then I'll do it."

♬ ♪ ♬ ♪ ♬

Late that morning, Hank heard footsteps on the porch. When he looked through the front window, he saw an adult with Down's Syndrome and a middle-aged woman. He opened the door. "Can I help you?"

"Is Mrs. Franklin home?" Megan asked.

"No, but I expect her any minute. Can I help you with something?"

"My name is Megan Morgan. I'm the director of the Arthur Hills Group Home where Mr. Fox lives," she said, looking at and nodding toward Dick Fox. "We were wondering if Mr. Spencer's dog, Aria, lives here?"

"We're taking care of Aria until a suitable home can be found," Hank replied.

Megan looked toward Dick and said, "This is Dick Fox. When Mr. Spencer was alive, Dick would walk Aria and feed her and just take care of her."

"I miss Aria," Dick said sadly.

"I'm sure you do," Hank said. "Would you like to come inside and see Aria?"

"That would be wonderful," Megan replied.

"Mrs. Franklin should be home any minute now. In the meantime, come in and visit Aria." Hank opened a door to the kitchen and Aria ambled out. As soon as she saw Dick she got all excited, wagged her tail, and ran to Dick, jumping up on him.

"Looks like Aria missed you, Dick."

Dick didn't respond. He knelt beside her and kept petting her and rubbing her ears.

Belle pulled into her driveway and wondered who was visiting. She went into the house where Hank introduced their guests. Belle greeted each with a handshake and a smile.

"Dick misses Aria and wanted to see her," Hank explained. "Dick used to help Mr. Spencer by walking Aria, feeding her, brushing, and petting her."

"I miss Aria," Dick said once again.

"I see." Belle looked at Dick and Aria. "They both seem happy together."

"Dick has been quite sad since Mr. Spencer died and you took Aria in."

"We'll do whatever we can to arrange visits till we find a good home for her. Perhaps you could adopt Aria?" Belle asked.

"Thank you, but we can't afford to have her. I'm the director of a group home where Dick lives with other men who have a variety of disabilities."

"I see." Belle directed her comment to Dick. "Sure was nice of you to help Mr. Spencer with Aria. I'm sure he appreciated your kindness."

Dick looked down at the floor, but then raised his head, looked at Belle and said, "He never paid me."

Megan just looked forlorn and shook her head.

"He agreed to pay you for caring for his dog?" Belle asked.

Megan jumped in, "Roland agreed to pay Dick fifty dollars a week to care for Aria, but he only actually paid on one or two occasions. I was furious with him, to put it mildly! How dare he take advantage of Dick?" Megan asked, her face getting red and her voice rising.

"Have you put a lien on his property?" Belle asked.

"What does that mean?" Megan asked.

"It means the executor of his estate would have to pay off the debt to Dick before selling the home."

"Would I need a lawyer to do this?" Megan asked.

"Yes, I imagine you would."

"We can't afford a lawyer."

"Did you have a contract with Roland?"

"No, he just said he would pay Dick fifty dollars a week."

"How long did Dick care for Aria without being paid?"

"At least three years."

"He never paid?" Belle asked.

"He paid once in a great while."

"Why didn't you advise Dick to stop providing this service?" Hank asked.

"I did, but he loves Aria. He couldn't imagine not walking her and feeding her. To Dick, it wasn't about the money."

"But to you, it was. Right?" Belle asked.

"Yes. Dick needs money for personal expenses. Every week I would tell Mr. Spencer he had to pay but he would just ignore me. I got so angry. One time I was so mad I almost passed out. That was wrong, taking advantage of a man with a disability."

"We agree. We'd be angry as well, but I think we'd simply stop the service," Hank replied.

"I love Aria," Dick said, continuing to pet and hug her.

"How about you and Dick taking Aria when you leave," Belle suggested. "We'll give you food, her leash, and we'll pay you fifty dollars a week till we find a home."

"Would you like to do that?" Megan asked Dick.

Dick smiled and wiped a tear of joy from his cheek.

♫ ♪ ♫ ♪ ♫

A week later, Belle called Megan to see when she could stop by and pay Dick for his work during the week. Megan suggested Belle come over anytime and she did. She walked into the group home, greeting the residents. Eventually, Megan appeared with a warm greeting.

Belle looked around the common room, noting a big screen television, a few well-worn lounge chairs and a bowl of peanuts. "Looks like a healthy snack," Belle remarked.

"These men go through a couple bags of chips a day. I had to put my foot down and provide something healthier."

"How long have the peanuts been in the bowl?" Belle asked.

"I fill the bowl about twice a week."

"I see. Well, here's a check for Dick's work," Belle said as she handed the money to Megan. "I assume he has a bank account?"

"Oh, yes. He counts his money like King Midas. Excuse me while I go to the kitchen and get my receipt book."

While Megan was gone, Belle walked over to the bowl of peanuts and put a few in her pocket. Megan returned, handed Belle a receipt, thanked her for coming over, and walked her to the front door.

"Oh, one more thing, if I may," Belle began. "Would you mind if I took a photo of you, Dick, and Aria?"

"I guess so. But why on earth would you want a picture of me?" Megan asked.

"The choir members are curious about what happened to Roland's dog. I'd like to show them she's being well-treated."

"I see. Dick isn't here right now."

"But, you and Aria are, so could I take a photo of you two? I can take a photo of Dick some other time."

"I guess that would be okay," Megan replied. She located Aria in the back yard, scooped her up, and returned to the front door. Belle snapped a good shot of the two.

"Thank you, Megan. I'll probably stop by again next week to pay Dick for his work."

"Thank you, Mrs. Franklin."

The Holy Living Waters Church's annual spring craft show was scheduled to begin on Friday, May 5. The vendors provided quality craftsmanship displayed in elaborate style. Each booth resembled a small store in a fashionable mall. Vendors from Michigan, Ohio, and Indiana applied for space at a rate of $350 for an eight-by-ten foot booth. The fee was waived for church members, which opened up space for additional vendors, such as Peggy Potts Peanut Brittle, the youth group's cookies, and the women's circle's cake walk.

The choir raised money for music, robes, and travel expenses by selling CDs of their favorite hymns. This year, the CDs were expected to sell well as the CD was Roland's last performance.

The Boy and Girl Scout troops sponsored by the church sold bags of peanuts and popcorn. Also included in their arsenal of goodies would be soft drinks priced triple what someone would pay in fast food eateries, but it was for charity and a good cause. The Krall sisters Betty, Linda, and Barbara would visit as they did every year, to spend a considerable sum of money on holiday gifts for birthdays, anniversaries, and weddings. They looked for everything from note cards to Easter bonnets with all the frills.

♫ ♪ ♫ ♪ ♫

Belle noted the entry for Peggy Potts Peanut Brittle and decided to phone Peggy, if for no other reason than that the word 'peanut' jumped out at her.

"Hi, Peggy. This is Belle Franklin."

"Yes, Belle."

"I see you're selling your peanut brittle again this year at the craft show."

"That's right. I have a lot of fans and people expect me to be there every year."

"You've a great-tasting treat, Peggy."

"Thanks. But you didn't call to talk to me about peanut brittle, did you?"

"No, I didn't. I'm trying to find out what exactly happened to Roland Spencer. The autopsy report noted that he died of anaphylaxis, his allergy to peanuts."

"So?"

"So, I wonder if you know of any connection between your candy and Roland."

"The only way Roland would have come in contact with my brittle is if someone had bought it and gave it to him."

"You don't recall him ever buying any himself?" Belle asked.

"No, I don't."

"Where do you get the peanuts, or is it a state secret?"

"Not a secret. I get big bags of them from Sam's Club."

"And you store them in your home until you make the brittle, I assume."

"Correct."

"Thanks, Peggy. No more questions."

"That's good news. I hope I'm off the hook."

"You were never on a hook, but I know what you mean." Belle needed to check off anyone associated with the crime, and peanuts fit Peggy Potts Peanut Brittle like a glove.

♫ ♪ ♫ ♪ ♫

Belle told Lou of her visit to the group home and Megan's intense anger against Roland, and the peanuts she lifted from the common room.

"Hmm, interesting. Another suspect to add to your list."

"I thought so too, but I have her at the end of the list."

"I'm talking about the man with the disability."

"Really? I don't think so."

"You have to consider all possibilities, Belle," Lou advised. "And, for the record, I am suggesting that perhaps the woman used the man to set up Roland's murder."

"Two suspects then? The woman acting alone, or the woman setting up the man with the disability."

"Yes."

"Okay. So, what is the next step for me?" Belle asked.

"You need to find out how someone dies of anaphylaxis," Lou replied. "So you need to interview a physician—perhaps an allergist, or pathologist."

"Makes sense."

Belle called the medical examiner for Washtenaw County, Linda Weiss. She was unavailable, so Belle left a message asking her to return the call. In the meantime, she typed "anaphylaxis" into the Google search engine on her computer; up popped 4 million sites. To learn as much as she could about this malady, Belle made notes and copied significant pages until her tired eyes demanded she stop.

♫ ♪ ♫ ♪ ♫

When an innocent-looking young man appeared on her porch several hours later, Belle opened the door. "Hello."

He smiled at her. "Hi, are you Isabelle Franklin?"

"Yes."

"I'm Bernie Higgins, Roland Spencer's 'little brother', from the Big Brother/Big Sister Program. When I was about eight years old, he volunteered to be my big brother, and I've never forgotten him. He was a nice man."

"I'm sure he was. Would you like to come in?" Belle asked.

"Thanks. I want to explain why I'm here."

"Come, sit in the living room. Can I get you some cookies and coffee?"

"No thanks, I really can't stay. When I heard that Roland had died, I grieved. A few days later I contacted the police, who told me that you were working with Mr. Searing to solve the crime."

"That's true, but we don't yet know for sure whether Roland's death was a crime. It could very well have been from natural causes. In fact, I've uncovered nothing yet that indicates that Roland was murdered."

"He was, Mrs. Franklin."

"He was?" Belle was astonished by such a firm statement.

"I'm sure of it, but I don't know how to prove it. So that's where you come in."

"I'm curious, as you can imagine," Belle replied. "How do you know it was murder?" Frustration showed on Bernie's face.

"He told me something that stuck with me."

"Can you tell me?" Belle asked.

"Yes. In graduate school, Roland was one of a small group of highly-intelligent chemists whose collective goal was to help preserve the environment. They formulated an environmentally safe chemical spray that, when applied on a lawn, would keep the grass green, but at the same time keep its height no more than a couple of inches."

"That would certainly be a gift to the environment," Belle said, thinking of the implications of such an invention.

"He would tell me about their theories and explain how those theories worked," Bernie explained.

"Did they ever complete the project?" Belle asked.

"Yes, but their results were never published because the unions and companies involved with lawn care smothered it. The lobbyists killed it before it reached final testing stages."

"Who were the other chemists, Bernie?"

"Roland was the creative genius of the group. I don't recall names, but I know there were two others and Roland talked about a chemistry professor who participated."

"I see. But what does this have to do with Roland's death?" Belle asked.

"Roland held a patent for the formula; the others were livid that he had applied for it behind their backs. Plus, the university professor knew that any patent applied for by a student, by law, must also list the university as the holder of the patent. Lots of anger and tension; lots of reasons to get Roland for his actions. Do you see?"

"Yes, but why would Roland be so selfish?" Belle asked.

"Because he knew that the invention could be worth billions and he was greedy."

"So you're suggesting that someone connected with this group killed him?"

"That's my reasoning," Bernie replied.

"But, how do you know all of this?" Belle asked.

"Even after I was finished with the Big Brother program, Roland and I maintained a friendship over the years. He would confide in me now and then."

"Would you recognize the others in a lineup?"

"I might recognize names, or maybe be able to pick them out of a lineup, but I couldn't be sure. I was pretty young, about eight at the time."

"Was this group in Chelsea?" Belle asked.

"I lived in Saline, but I know it was somewhere around Ann Arbor."

"Might one or more of them have been at the University of Michigan or Eastern Michigan University?"

"That's logical, but I really don't know which, if either."

"This is pretty crazy. Graduate-school chemists developing a formula to eliminate the need to mow lawns, golf courses, and a host of landscapes. Sounds like science fiction. Are you sure this really happened?"

"Well, these guys were odd, I mean, really odd. I'll swear on a stack of Bibles it's true."

"Okay, stranger things have happened, I suppose," Belle said, trying her best to accept the story. "At any rate, you don't know their names or where I could find them?"

"Sorry."

"Did Roland ever take you to one of their meetings, or to a laboratory?"

"Yes."

"Do you remember where it was?"

"It wasn't on a campus, but in a home, and I'm guessing probably in Ann Arbor."

"I'll look into it, Bernie," Belle said.

"Okay. I'm just trying to help, is all."

"Did your mom or dad know Roland?"

"I was a 'little brother' because my parents were divorced. I lived with my father, but I don't think my dad and Roland ever met. Roland would pull in the drive and beep the horn to let me know he was at the house and waiting for me to come to the car. I don't recall Dad talking to him."

"Okay, thanks. Your story could very well be pertinent, and I will look into it. Before you leave, let me repeat it, so I have it right. Roland filed for a patent in his name only, even though there were others who created the formula with him."

"That's it in a nutshell."

"Okay, thanks for stopping by. Here's my card in case you need to contact me."

"I hope you find out what happened, Mrs. Franklin."

"I will, I just need to find the facts to make sense of it all. Oh, Bernie, before you go, please look at this photograph. Do you recognize the woman or the dog?"

"No, sorry. Who are they?" Bernie asked.

"The dog was Roland's pug, and the woman directs a group home for disabled men in Roland's neighborhood."

"Cute pug. No, I've never seen either of them."

♫ ♪ ♫ ♪ ♫

Bernie's visit made Belle realize she'd have to dig deeper into Roland's past to solve the mystery. She called Lou to tell him what Bernie had said.

"Boy, that's a new one," Lou replied, after hearing Belle recount Bernie's story.

"There's no reason for this guy to lie to me, but I have trouble accepting his story, Lou."

"I know, but you can run with parts of it, at least for awhile."

"Parts of it?" Belle asked.

"Roland being selfish and greedy is logical," Lou offered. "Lots of people are that way."

"Yes, but a compound to cap the height grass would grow?" Belle asked, astonished.

"For now, I'd try to find these associates from years ago and see what, if anything, they have to say."

"Okay, Lou. You're my mentor; I'll follow your lead."

"Good. I think we must give this young man the benefit of the doubt, at least until we find out that he's out in left field. But who knows? This could be quite relevant."

♫ ♪ ♫ ♪ ♫

Belle went to talk with a pathologist at Chelsea Hospital on Monday afternoon, May 1. Belle had explained her purpose over the phone, so Dr. Harriet Kazyak was prepared to help.

The doctor began with a technical analysis. "Anaphylaxis. The definition I like to use is 'a serious allergic reaction, rapid in onset, that may cause death.' Anaphylaxis can be divided into 'true anaphylaxis', 'pseudo anaphylaxis', and 'anaphylactoid reaction'. The symptoms, treatment, and risk of death are the same; however, 'true' anaphylaxis is caused by degranulation of mast cells, or basophils, mediated by immunoglobulin E, or IgE, and pseudo-anaphylaxis occurs without IgE mediation."

"Whoa, whoa! You're way over my head," Belle exclaimed, interrupting the explanation. "I don't need a med school course; please, I just need to know the circumstances that might explain Roland's death."

"Sorry. I thought you needed a detailed explanation."

"Oh, no. Since Roland was brought here from the church, and the autopsy was done here, do you have any specifics about the cause of death besides the broad term, anaphylaxis?"

"Yes, I consulted his file before you arrived."

"Is anaphylaxis always caused by an allergy to peanuts?" Belle asked.

"Heavens, no! A peanut is just one of a great many allergens. Granted, it is the most common, and people are generally more aware of it, but there are many other allergens."

Belle continued taking notes—jotting down what she could understand of Dr. Kazyak's explanations and what she thought Lou would want to know.

When she was out of questions, Belle extended her hand. "Thank you Dr. Kazyak. I feel as if I just audited a class at U of M, but I have a better grasp of Roland's possible cause of death."

"Glad I could help."

Belle stepped toward the door, then quickly turned back. "Oh, one more question, if I may."

"Certainly."

"I recently learned something about Roland that might provide a motive for murder, but I'm almost convinced it's completely impossible."

"Explain, please."

"Apparently Roland studied chemistry in graduate school—probably at U of M or EMU. He, along with a small group of fellow students, synthesized environmentally-friendly chemicals that limited grass growth to a couple of inches. Any thoughts?" Belle asked.

"Well, I imagine it's possible, and it's probably been invented by now, but I know nothing about such a compound or its development. Do you mean artificial sod, like Astroturf?"

"No. Apparently the chemical was meant to be sprayed on living grass."

"Sorry, I've never heard of this."

"Okay, thanks. You've been very helpful."

"You're welcome. I'm not a forensic pathologist," Dr. Kazyak continued, but I'm amazed at what chemical engineers do these days. Someone with those credentials would be of much more help to you."

"For now, you were just what I needed, and I appreciate your time and knowledge."

♫ ♪ ♫ ♪ ♫

Friday, May 5 was the opening day for the Holy Living Waters Church Craft Show. The church gym was full of crafters from Chelsea and other Michigan cities, and even some from Indiana and Ohio. Peggy and her peanut brittle were in her usual spot by the front door. Choir members were selling copies of their CD, *Joyous Moments in Song*. Every craft imaginable seemed to be represented. Directly under the basketball hoop, Tim and Teresa Traxler sold their specialty handbags and purses designed by Jordan McMillan in Texas. They were attractive, expensive, and would only be of interest to those shoppers with money.

Belle was taken aback by a sign in the Traxler booth:

CLUE

A HANDBAG WILL BE PRESENTED
TO EACH 'DETECTIVE' WHO SOLVES
THE MURDER OF ROLAND SPENCER.

*Simply write on your entry form who killed
Roland in the choir loft and how.*

What is this? Belle thought. *Are they making fun of Roland's death? Do they know something I don't? Probably not, but why use the death of a man in our choir in a game of chance?*

Belle walked over to the booth and asked to speak with Teresa, privately. The two retreated to a quiet corner.

"What are you doing, Teresa? Surely, you don't know how Roland died, or who killed him?"

"Maybe we do, and maybe we don't," Teresa said smugly.

"Is this a joke?" Belle asked, shaking her head.

"No. We'll hold all entries until the case is solved, and then we'll give a purse to each winner. I mean, it happened in the choir loft, and someone did it. Our contest is like the childhood game CLUE."

"You suppose you'll see, 'The minister did it in the choir loft with a gun,'? or something like that?" Belle asked.

"Exactly! We're just having fun."

"At Roland's expense?" Belle asked sharply.

"It might surprise you to know that Tim and I were friends of Roland's. And I know for a fact that Roland would fully endorse our humor."

"'For a fact?'" Belle asked. "Those are pretty strong words. Are you implying that you discussed this scheme with Roland before his death?"

"In a way, yes."

"What do you mean?"

"Roland predicted his own death. It is sort of eerie how he knew details."

"Please explain." Belle was almost speechless.

"We were having coffee after dinner and the conversation switched to when we might die."

"Kind of a morbid conversation," Belle replied.

"True, but Tim mentioned that, with his birthday next week, he is mid-way between the ages of his mother when she died and his father when he died. Then Roland said something like, 'I know how, when, and where I will die.'

"We were astonished and didn't believe him. But, Roland was quite off-hand about it. In fact, he was right about at least one of the how, who, and where questions. We'll just have to wait till the 'how' and 'who' become known."

"He said he would die in the choir loft?" Belle repeated.

"Yes."

"So, do you know who killed him?" Belle asked.

"No, we don't know that, Belle." Teresa sounded annoyed.

"Why would you keep this information from the police?" Belle asked, astonished at Teresa's manner. If you know anything about Roland's death, you may be withholding evidence."

"The police haven't asked us anything. How can we possibly be withholding something we haven't even been asked about?" Teresa asked, smiling at Belle.

"You know I'm investigating Roland's death. Surely, you'll tell me," Belle said.

"You're not the police, Belle," Teresa responded tersely.

"I realize that, but I'm asking point-blank: Do you know how Roland died?"

"I'll take the Fifth," Teresa replied as she turned her back on Belle and headed toward her booth.

♫ ♪ ♫ ♪ ♫

Belle sought out Reverend Norris and told him about the Traxler's contest.

"I can't believe Tim and Teresa would do something like this," Belle began.

"I agree, but while we don't agree with their choice, they have a right to make it." The Reverend sounded resigned.

"Can you talk to them and see if you can learn any more what they know of Roland's death?" Belle asked.

"I will."

Reverend Norris contacted Tim, who came to the church office during his lunch break. "Well, you certainly have Belle's attention, Tim."

"I gather she's not happy with our CLUE contest."

"She thinks it unfortunate that you're making a game out of this tragedy. She's trying to find the truth and she can't understand why you won't come forth with anything that might help solve the case. Why withhold information? is her question."

"We understand that."

"Do you and Teresa really know what happened to Roland? Because if you do, you're walking down a path you really don't want to take."

"What do you mean?" Tim asked.

"Belle is not qualified to do police work. She is looking into this because she is suspect and wants an explanation. My point is, if Belle believes you are withholding information, she will inform the police. It could lead to charges against you. I'm sure you don't want that to happen."

"I'll tell you the truth, Reverend."

"Thank you, but you need to tell Belle."

"I will, but in advance of that, we know nothing. We were simply using the idea as a pitch to get customers into our booth."

"By propagating a lie? Your wife said Roland told you details about his upcoming death. She was lying to Belle?"

"That's right."

"So you, like the rest of us, don't have a clue, pun intended, as to how, why, who, or anything else about Roland's death," Reverend Norris replied.

"That's correct."

"I won't hesitate to tell you, this was hardly a Christian thing to do."

"I understand."

"As your pastor, I demand that you end your contest and explain your deception to anyone who asks you why the contest is off."

"I'm sorry for the trouble this has caused." Tim appeared genuinely remorseful.

"I accept your apology. I also ask that you give me all of the forms put into your CLUE box."

"Teresa or I will stop by with all of the entries, but nobody's guessing. I say, 'all' but we only have a few."

While the Chelsea police weren't prioritizing the Roland Spencer case, they did have it on their radar. Chief Purdy was confident that, with Lou Searing involved, he needn't allocate extra staff and resources to the investigation.

The detective assigned to the case was Derrick Thomas, a 25-year veteran who had solved several crimes in his career. Most of his energy was currently invested in a most difficult case; to get his mind off that crime, he would occasionally spend some time looking into the Spencer case. He, like many others, was convinced that the cause of death was not murder. He opened the Spencer file and quickly scanned several pages, then asked to speak with Chief Purdy.

"I can't help but put this choir director at the top of my list of suspects," Detective Thomas began. "She went to the store before going back to the church, so, I stopped at the grocery to ask a few questions."

"For example?"

"The first thing was, what did she buy?"

"And, did they know?" Chief Purdy asked.

"Yes, as a matter of fact they did. Their system keeps track of all purchases to provide accountability, help with inventory, and make tax-filing simple."

"They even know the name of the person buying the items?" Chief Purdy asked with skepticism.

"No, but I talked to the cashier, and she recalled some of the items this Mrs. Franklin bought. It was easy to find the receipt because the time of purchase is also recorded."

"So, what did she buy—bread and milk?"

"As a matter of fact, she did. But she also bought ice cream, celery, a liter of diet cola, and—this is what brings her under the microscope—peanuts, and a magazine titled *True Crime*," Detective Thomas replied with a smile.

"That's an odd collection for someone running to the store in the evening," Chief Purdy remarked. "We might presume that she did not go into the church as she claims."

"The ice cream, right?"

"Exactly. She needed to go right home or have a melted mess on her hands. I've a hunch. I'm going over to the church to check something out."

Chief Purdy drove to the church, left his vehicle in the lot, and went to the church office to request permission to look around in the kitchen.

"What's the government doing now?" the church secretary, Mrs. Sneath, asked annoyed at being interrupted. "Giving our men in blue the responsibility of monitoring health codes?"

"I need to check something on the Spencer case."

"You know where the kitchen is," Mrs. Sneath replied as she went back to her bookkeeping.

"Thanks. You'll let Reverend Norris know I'm here?"

"Sure," Mrs. Sneath replied. "He'll probably come join you in the kitchen. His curiosity can't keep him away."

Chief Purdy left the office and headed downstairs to the kitchen. He turned on the lights and walked around looking for anything out of the ordinary. Four upright freezers stood side by side; he needed to check all of them. When he opened the second, he found what he sought: a half-gallon of Mackinac Island Fudge ice cream.

Just then, Reverend Norris appeared in the open doorway. "Good morning, Chief. Hungry?"

"No, just working on a hunch."

"Which is?"

"Mrs. Franklin said she stopped here on her way home from the grocery store. Purchase records show that she bought ice cream. If she did stop here, the ice cream would have melted in her car; but she could have brought it into the church, where it would make sense to put it in the freezer. It appears that she did just that."

"Yes, staff members often use our facilities for personal reasons," Reverend Norris continued. "But why put ice cream in the freezer if all she was doing was checking to see if Roland was in the church?"

"That action implies she planned to stay longer," reasoned the chief.

"I'm just the pastor, officer—you're the pro—but I don't think you can connect the ice cream to Belle. No one saw her put it in there. Her name isn't on it. Do the store records note the flavor of ice cream?"

"No, the item is only noted as 'Dairy, ice cream'."

"Far be it from me to judge, but I do know that particular flavor is our janitor's favorite."

"This is the guy who carried around the peanuts—the guy who discovered the body?"

"Yes. His name is Winston Saturn."

"Maybe we should look at him as a potential suspect."

"He wouldn't hurt a fly, but you could talk to him," replied Reverend Norris.

"Is there anything he and Roland had in common?"

"Nothing I can think of, but I don't make it a practice to know what people do after work hours."

"They never talked about golf, or bowling, or anything?" Chief Purdy asked.

"Now that you mention it, I did hear them comment on their gambling."

"Gambling?"

"You know, a buck on a Sunday ball game, or something like that."

"I see. I don't know who this ice cream belongs to, but I'll have to take it back to the station and enter it as evidence."

"I'd appreciate your putting a note to this effect on the outside freezer door. If the owner finds the ice cream missing, accusations will fly, and you could have your second murder in our church."

"You said 'murder'; do you know that it was murder?"

"No, I don't. I jumped to a conclusion; I take it back."

Chief Purdy noted the miscue, if in fact it was one.

♫ ♪ ♫ ♪ ♫

When Chief Purdy got back to the station, he called Lou to report what he had found and to discuss his conversation with Reverend Norris.

Armed with the information Chief Purdy had given him, Lou called Belle.

"Got a minute?" Lou asked

"For you, I have hours," Belle replied. "What've you got?"

"The night Roland died, you went to the grocery store, then stopped back at the church on the way home. Do you recall that?" Lou asked.

"Like it happened an hour ago."

"Do you recall what you bought?" Lou asked.

"Now, that'll be a challenge. I'm one of those who goes frequently for a few items. Let's see, that was a Wednesday night, so I probably got some bananas, milk, bread, apples, and caramels. Hank likes apples, but he loves them with caramels."

"How about ice cream?" Lou asked. "Did you buy any?"

"Oh, no. Are you kidding? That's banned in our home."

"Are you sure?"

"Positive!"

"Hmm, the Chelsea Police say the grocery store retrieval system shows you purchased ice cream."

"Well, they have it wrong, Lou. The man in front of me bought ice cream."

"You remember that?"

"When the guy was checking out he noticed that he had strawberry, and asked the check-out person if he could go back and get Mackinac Island Fudge. Needless to say, people in line were not happy to wait for him. I even recall helping to keep the peace, urging folks to relax."

"How did you pay for your groceries?" Lou asked.

"Cash."

"I'll have the store check their receipts—they'll have another from that evening."

"If they doubt me, they can come to my home and look in my freezer."

"They may. I can't know what they will or won't do with their information. The theory is that you took the ice cream into the church and put it in the freezer in the kitchen because if you had left it in your car, it would have melted and created quite a mess."

"I was only in the church two minutes, or the equivalent of a mile on the road. I'm sure an entire carton of ice cream would not melt in two minutes."

"You supposedly knew you'd be longer in the church…"

"While I killed Roland, right?" Belle said, interrupting Lou.

"That's the thinking, yes."

"I understand their theory, but it doesn't work. I left my groceries in the car because nothing was going to spoil. I went into the church, walked around turning on lights and calling Roland's name. When I heard no response, I turned off the lights and left."

"I just had a brief premonition, Belle."

"I love premonitions. Tell me."

"Could Reverend Norris be a suspect?" Lou asked.

"Not a prayer, Lou. He is the most upstanding gentleman I have ever met."

"Whoa, give me a chance to explain. He had keys to the church. He had had a confrontation with Roland. Seems like a perfect way to set you up, or Phyllis, or the janitor, while claiming innocence."

"I see what you mean. I guess he could've done it, but he'd be the last person on my list of suspects. I'm that confident, Lou."

"Fine. It was a hunch, and it's probably far from the truth. Not all of my notions are valid, but I pay attention to them when I get them. And, while I am on hunches, that woman walking her dog walking down the street as you returned to the church, what is that about?"

"It looked innocent," Belle replied.

"Who was she? What did the dog look like?"

"I'm not even sure it was a woman. The dog was a dog."

"Yes, but a big dog, little dog, shaggy dog, a dog with big ears, little ears..."

"Sorry, Lou. Put me under hypnosis and I might be able to help more, but all I remember is a normal-sized woman and a normal-sized dog."

"Okay, the more you get into this investigative stuff, the better you get at noticing details."

"I hope so."

"One more question about the woman. Did she look like she had just come out of the church? Did she look back toward the church at any time?"

"No, she was just walking down the sidewalk, and I didn't see her look back."

♫ ♪ ♫ ♪ ♫

Belle needed to go downtown to have her hair done, so she decided to stop at the police station afterward and talk to Chief Purdy.

"Hello, Chief. How is the protector of our town's safety doing today?"

"It's a full-moon day."

"What's that mean?" Belle asked.

"An old wives' tale, but there seems to be some truth to it. When the moon is full, all kinds of crazy things happen. If you talk to people in hospitals, law enforcement, teachers… they'll tell you that during the full moon, unexpected things happen."

"Hmm. I'd not heard of that."

"As I say, it's an old wives' tale. But, it offers an explanation for craziness."

"I have choir practice tonight. I'll have to see if your full-moon theory creeps into my practice."

"Oh, it will." replied Chief Purdy. "Anyway, what can I do for you, Mrs. Franklin?"

"Lou Searing told me that I'm a suspect in the Spencer death. Someone thinks I bought ice cream, and put it in the church freezer. I'd have time to kill Roland and still have frozen ice cream."

"It was just a thought."

"Well, Chief, there isn't a spoonful of truth to it," Belle said. "And furthermore, in the future if you have a theory about me, please show me the courtesy of sharing it with me first. Let's keep the communication channels open. After all, we're both trying to accomplish the same goal."

"Okay. Sorry to offend you," Chief Purdy said.

"Happens, but it doesn't need to. Oh—and for the record—I did not buy ice cream that evening, and I did not kill Roland. Understood?" Belle asked, straightening up to her full height.

"I got the message, Belle."

♫ ♪ ♫ ♪ ♫

When Belle got home, she listened to a message left on her phone.

"Mrs. Franklin. This is Bernie Higgins, Roland Spencer's little brother. Remember we talked before? Anyway, I have a photo of Roland and his chemistry friends. Do you want it? Please call or e-mail me, and I'll get it to you."

Immediately, Belle returned the call to let Bernie know that she definitely wanted the photo. Bernie agreed to bring it over within the hour.

"Thank you. This may be an important piece in the puzzle of Roland's death."

"I hope so. See you in a few minutes."

♫ ♪ ♫ ♪ ♫

Bernard Higgins never arrived. Belle called him again, but there was no answer. She drove to his home. No car was in the driveway, and no one appeared to be home. *Maybe this is part of that full-moon thing Chief Purdy was talking about,* Belle thought.

She drove home hoping to find Bernie waiting on her porch. He was not there nor was there an explanatory note, nor a further message on the phone. She needed to be at the church for choir practice at seven, but she would be close to the phone until she had to leave. At ten to seven, she taped a note on the door telling Bernie where she was, in case he stopped by.

With the full moon on her mind, Belle went to the music room for voice warm-ups and announcements before leading everyone to the choir loft. Just as the choir was about to sing the Doxology, a distraught and pale Reverend Norris appeared before his angelic singers.

Reverend Norris approached Belle, speaking softly. "May I see you in the morning, Belle?"

"Why wait till morning?" she replied. "Can we talk now?"

"I suppose so. Let's go to my office."

Belle turned the rehearsal over to Tom Everlast, who often led the choir in Belle's absence.

Once they were comfortably seated in the Reverend's soft red leather chairs, Reverend Norris began, "How do you think the investigation is going, Belle?"

"Well, it is not going quickly."

"Yes. I guess you've heard that word on the street is that you are responsible for Roland's death."

"That's unfortunate, because nothing is further from the truth!" Belle blurted out.

Reverend Norris sat quietly with his hands folded, as if in prayer. After a pause he looked at Belle and said, "I'm sorry but I must suggest you leave your position in the church until this is settled."

"You can't be serious!" Belle retorted.

"Yes, I'm afraid I am. For good or ill, your presence disturbs several members who think you either killed Roland or had a part in his killing."

"Don't I have rights here?" Belle asked, becoming more agitated. "Like, innocent until proven guilty?"

"I checked with our attorney. You are a contract employee, and therefore, you can be terminated for any reason. I'm not asking you to leave, I'm only asking you to step out of the spotlight till things quiet a bit."

"Step out of the spotlight?" Belle said, her voice rising. "That's how you see me? In a spotlight? Honestly, Reverend Norris, what ever happened to supporting the people who contribute their talents to your congregation?"

"Let's not get testy here, Belle."

"I'm not getting testy," Belle shot back angrily. "You remove me from my choir because you think I'm 'in the spotlight'. Instead, couldn't you say something like, 'The congregation and I believe Mrs. Franklin should not be the subject of rumors and innuendo. She is innocent in our eyes, and we're proud to have her in our congregation.' Would that have been out of place?"

"You've a good point there," Reverend Norris said realizing he had acted rashly. "The Chief suggested I remove you from the employ of the church because people are talking. I want to support our police chief. If he thinks your absence would help solve the mystery, I feel obliged to follow his lead. Of course, you have nothing to do with this. We know that."

"Well then, show some integrity! Stand up for what you believe!" Belle was almost breathless now.

"I apologize, Belle. Please stay, and together we'll get through this."

Belle took a deep breath, realizing that Reverend Norris had changed his position. "I accept your apology, Reverend Norris, and I will continue to direct the choir."

"Thank you. I guess the stress is getting to me. They never told us in seminary how to handle a death in the choir loft."

"I'd hope seminary professors would not waste time doing so," Belle replied.

They rose, shook hands, and Belle left the office. She walked back to the choir loft and resumed rehearsal as though nothing had happened.

♫ ♪ ♫ ♪ ♫

When Belle arrived home following choir practice, there was a folded note on her door. *Great,* she thought, *Bernie has been here with the information about Roland.* She took the note from the door, walked into the house and headed to the phone to check messages. The message light was blinking; she pushed the code. She heard Lou's voice: "Hi Belle, please call me whenever you get this message. It is important that I talk with you."

Belle dialed Lou's number. Lou answered immediately. "Thank you for calling, Belle. What I have to say could have waited till tomorrow, but I want to know what you learned about the prescription."

"Prescription? I'm not following."

"You told me that a doctor's prescription was tucked into Roland's music folder."

"Oh, yes, there was."

"I trust you looked into this?"

"No, I didn't, Lou," Belle said, chagrined. "Sorry."

"There could be something important in that, Belle. I'm not being judgmental, only doing my job as a mentor."

"I want you to be critical—how else can I learn? I'll get right on that."

"Let me know what you find out."

"I will. Thanks, Lou. Oh, one more thing. Reverend Norris told me this evening that I should remove myself as the choir director and organist, saying I needed to be out of the spotlight."

"I want you to be in the 'spotlight'," Lou replied forcefully. "It keeps the case in the public eye. Don't be offended. That is precisely what I want."

"OK. But, I raised such an objection I sent him on a guilt trip, and he changed his mind."

"Good. All's well then."

Belle put the phone down and gave her full attention to the note. The hand-written message was brief but definitive: "Bernie has nothing to say. He was mistaken in thinking he could help you with your investigation."

Belle sensed immediately that the opposite was true, that Bernie could share something, and it could be helpful to have in hand. She tried repeatedly to reach Bernie by phone and by e-mail, but she received no response.

♫ ♪ ♫ ♪ ♫

Belle couldn't believe that she'd forgotten the prescription in Roland's music folder. Winston had set the page on her desk, and Belle had put it in a secure drawer. The next morning she retrieved it and made arrangements to see Dr. Jerome Worthy.

When she hung up, Belle decided to look carefully through everything in the music folder. The first thing she saw was a sealed business envelope with her name written neatly on the front. Opening the envelope, she read:

> *Mrs. Franklin,*
>
> *While I have no expectation of leaving this earth anytime soon, I want you to know which hymns I'd like sung at my funeral. Of course, this is assuming I die while still living in Chelsea, and you are still the church organist and choir director. The hymns are as follows: "The Church is One Foundation", "Silent Night", and "Let There Be Peace on Earth".*

♫ ♪ ♫ ♪ ♫

"Could you please tell me what this prescription is for?" Belle asked, handing Roland's prescription to Dr. Worthy.

"Well, it could be for any number of symptoms, really. But I would most likely prescribe it to treat an emergency reaction to some allergen."

"Like the body's reaction to a bee sting?"

"Yes, or an asthmatic attack brought on by something the patient is severely allergic to."

"Like a bee sting or peanuts," Belle said.

"Yes, exactly. The patient was probably allergic to peanuts, and would show symptoms of anaphylaxis. If symptoms were present, the patient would be advised to take this medicine."

"But, he never submitted the prescription to the pharmacy," Belle noted.

"Apparently. What's the date on it?" Dr. Worthy asked.

"April 15."

"And he died when?"

"April 19."

"That means that he saw his doctor on the 15th. Or at least that his doctor wrote the prescription on that date," Dr. Worthy explained. "He could have called for a prescription and picked it up without seeing the doctor."

"Either way, getting the prescription meant either he was out of the last batch, or he needed it at the time it was written."

"Correct," replied Dr. Worthy.

"So, he didn't get the prescription filled, and he died a few days after it was written. He may have encountered a substance that triggered an allergic reaction, and without this medication handy, he could have died."

"That's possible, yes."

"Thank you, Doctor Worthy. By the way, it is nice to talk with you when I'm well!"

"Yes. You look very healthy, Belle. Keep on doing whatever you're doing."

"Really? So you're officially condoning my daily love affair with chocolate?"

"No comment," Dr. Worthy replied, smiling.

♫ ♪ ♫ ♪ ♫

Belle decided to stay close to home for several reasons. She wanted to be home in case Bernie might stop by with the photo. Although it angered her, she agreed Reverend Norris had a good point about her staying out of the public eye for a while. She thought about skipping choir rehearsal, asking Tom Eastman to fill in for her, but she decided she should be on the job, despite her being in that proverbial spotlight.

Belle drove to the church, parked, and went directly to the choir room, greeting many of the choir members. She gathered her music, and entered the loft via a door behind the organ. On the organ's music desk was a photo of a younger, thinner Roland with two other college-aged men. *This must be the photo from Bernie, but, how had it appeared on the organ?* Belle thought.

Turning the photo over, Belle read scratchy handwriting on the back: "Three brilliant chemists: Roland, Ted, and Blake, 1987." Now she needed to find Ted and Blake.

Usually choir practice was enjoyable, but tonight every minute seemed like an hour. She felt she had a mission, and it had nothing to do with music. She cut practice short by fifteen minutes and didn't stay at the church any longer than necessary.

When she got home she logged onto the Internet and typed "University Chemistry Departments in Michigan" into the search bar. Among many viable options were the departments at the University of Michigan, Eastern Michigan University, and Wayne State University. At each of these sites she visited the "Faculty" pages and quickly skimmed the lists looking for a "Theodore" or a "Blake". None appeared at any of the three universities. Next she searched "Chemists Associations", and up came some other options that she hoped might produce a name. The roadblock was that access to many of the sites was limited to members.

Frustrated, she called Lou. "I need your help."

"What can I do for you, Belle?"

"I have a photo of Roland and his chemist friends, Ted and Blake. On the Web, I searched local Universities and Chemist Associations and came up empty. How do I go about finding a Ted or a Blake who were chemistry students 25 years ago?"

"Well, I usually team up with Jack Kelly and he works his magic. But Jack is on a church mission in Mexico, and I don't want to bother him."

"Of course not," Belle replied. "I wouldn't expect you to."

"Let's see. You could check yearbooks. Have you narrowed your search area at all?"

"My source thinks they were in the Ann Arbor area."

"U of M, EMU are the obvious ones," Lou replied.

"And, University of Detroit, Wayne State University, and Oakland University as well," Belle added.

"Yes. You're looking for a known needle in several haystacks. It just takes grunt work and a lot of the right questions."

"It just hit me, Lou: maybe Roland had a yearbook or two in his home. It's a long shot, but I'd hate to spend months tracking down a yearbook with pictures of Roland, Blake, and Ted, only to find that what I wanted was in his home the whole time."

"Well, that's detective work. And nobody claims it's easy. Television shows where the actors solve the crime in an hour are a long way from how the process really works, Belle."

"Okay, Lou, gotta get to work. Thanks for your help."

07

That night as she tried to go to sleep, Belle kept thinking of Reverend Norris. She recalled Lou wondering if he should be a suspect and her defending the Reverend, saying what a fine and upstanding member of the community he was. Maybe he was the guilty party. He had keys to the church, he lived a short distance away, he knew the choir would be practicing. And she recalled his encounter with Roland, when Roland embarrassed him by not showing up at the charity event.

She knew that sometimes the one person everyone would think is innocent turns out to be guilty. She'd be sure to talk with Reverend Norris the next day. With that, Belle was able to the put the case aside and fall asleep.

The next morning, before heading out to the University of Michigan, Belle called and asked for an appointment with Reverend Norris. She could see him at 11:10 a.m.

Belle drove to Ann Arbor. Once inside the Chemistry Department, she introduced herself to the student receptionist. "I would like to talk to any faculty member who was here twenty-five years ago. Can you help me?" Belle asked.

"Hmm. Let me see whom I can find." The young woman disappeared into a long hallway lined with offices left and right. After an absence of about five minutes she reappeared with a distinguished-looking, grey-haired woman. Belle took a second glance, thinking she was seeing a reincarnation of Einstein.

"Can I help you? I'm Gladys Stout. I was here twenty-five years ago."

"I hope you can." Belle showed her the photo of the three young men. "This picture is of Roland, Ted, and Blake—I only have first names. Do you recognize any of them?"

"I had this student in one of my lab classes," Professor Stout replied, studying the photo and pointing to Roland. "But the other two I've never seen before."

"Is there another professor who was here then?"

"Professor Marcia Handley."

"May I talk with her?" Belle asked.

"I think she's in her office—please follow me." As Professor Stout led the way down the office-lined hallway, she asked, "Why are you looking for these men?"

Belle toyed with a lie, that she was doing a research project and needed to verify the results of some study. But, true to her personality, she was honest. "The one you recognized, Roland

Spencer? He died recently, and I'm trying to figure out how and why."

"So you're a detective?"

"I suppose a 'green-behind-the-ears detective' would best describe me," admitted Belle.

"Ah. Here we are." The two turned into an open office, where Professor Handley sat at her desk. "Marcia, this is Belle Franklin," Professor Stout said. "She's looking for a couple of former students. I thought you might be able to help."

Professor Handley rose from her chair, smiled, and shook Belle's hand. Her office was small and too full of books for a set of chairs. "Good morning. I hope I can help."

Professor Handley took the photo, stared at it for a few seconds, then blurted out, "I certainly will never forget these highly intelligent men. I predicted that if they were serious in their study of chemistry, they would be famous."

Pointing to Roland she said, "This is Roland Spencer. As I recall, he was a singer. One of my best students." She pointed to another, "This is Ted Waters. Ted had the personality of a mad professor. He went on to get his doctorate at the University of Iowa, and he's kept in touch. He works for Dow Chemical in Midland."

"How about this last one?" Belle asked, pointing to the third chemist.

"Blake Schooley: unfortunately, he died in a lab explosion at the University of Wisconsin a couple of years ago. If I recall correctly, a mixture exploded, killing him instantly. I saw both Roland and Ted at his funeral. They were pretty shaken by the tragedy, as I recall."

"So it looks like I need to contact Ted at Dow Chemical," Belle replied.

"You should find him there. In fact, I can give you his phone number if you'd like."

"Yes, thank you very much. You've been very helpful."

Armed with Ted's name and number, Belle left for Chelsea and her appointment with Reverend Norris.

♫ ♪ ♫ ♪ ♫

Just after Belle left, Professor Handley called Ted Waters. "I've got a 'heads up' for you, Ted. A woman from Chelsea just paid me a visit. She has a photo of you, Roland, and Blake. Apparently she's looking into Roland's death. I answered her questions and identified the three of you in the photo. She didn't ask anything else, but I knew you would want to be aware that she now knows who you are and where to find you."

"Thanks for calling. I think I'll plan a trip to California for a conference."

Ted disconnected, then rerecorded his telephone message. "Please leave a message. I'm currently attending a conference in California and may stay for an extended visit. I check my phone frequently and will return calls as time permits."

Belle heard that message when she dialed the number while driving back to Chelsea. She left a message for Dr. Ted Waters to please call her.

♫ ♪ ♫ ♪ ♫

Reverend Norris had no idea what Belle had on her mind. He couldn't come up with a reason to meet, except maybe to brief him on her quiet investigation.

At eleven o'five, Belle sat in a comfortable chair awaiting her appointment. She was always on time. Reverend Norris appeared at the door. "Belle, please come in."

"Thank you, Reverend, for fitting me into your schedule."

"You're welcome. You're important to me Belle. What can I do for you?" Reverend Norris asked, offering her the leather chair across from him.

"I know you're busy so let me cut to the chase. Where were you the evening Roland Spencer died?" Belle asked, pen held above her notepad.

"What is this, the third degree? Am I on the witness stand?" he asked, surprised.

"No offense. I'm talking with anyone who might have been in the church—or who could have access to the church—that evening."

"I fit both of those criteria, Belle. I was in my office working on my sermon during your choir practice. Actually, I usually work on my sermon then—I love the music. It relaxes me and creates an atmosphere for putting my thoughts on paper."

"Did you stay in your office when our practice ended, or did you work beyond our practice time?"

"I stayed on. What is this about, Belle? I'm disturbed you're treating me like a suspect. I had nothing to do with Roland's passing, and I resent your questioning me like this."

"I'm simply asking a few questions, Reverend. Did you leave your office after our rehearsal?"

"Yes, I left my office for a few minutes."

"To do what?" Belle asked.

"If you must know, I went to the bathroom. Then I went to the kitchen for some ice cream before coming back here to finish the sermon."

"Then, to the best of your recollection, you did not go to the choir loft between the end of practice and the next morning when Roland's body was discovered?"

"That's correct, and I see that my next appointment is here." Reverend Norris was visibly upset. "I trust you have all of the information you need? And, Belle, the next time you decide to interrogate me, please find some time when I am not trying to minister to a church member. Can I count on that?"

"As you wish. I view you on a par with any other member of the church, but obviously you don't. Furthermore, you seem uncomfortable discussing this with me. There must be a reason, but for now, thanks for your time."

Belle took the photo of Megan and Aria from her purse, showed it to Reverend Norris and asked, "Have you seen either this woman or this dog?"

"I've seen the dog. In fact I saw this dog in the foyer during a previous choir practice. I just figured Roland had brought his dog to rehearsal. I didn't appreciate the dog in the church, but I let it go."

"Was this before Roland died?" Belle asked.

"I don't know when it was. I am sure it was before, if it was Roland's dog."

"Can you try to recall when you saw Aria in church?"

"It had to have been the week that my sermon was on the importance of trust. I remember putting in a paragraph about how pets trust their owners to care for them. I keep all of my sermons on file and I date them. I'll look."

A moment later, the Reverend turned from the file cabinet and said, "The dog was in the church the week of April 16."

"Thank you, Reverend."

Reverend Norris nodded, opened the door to escort Belle out before inviting in his next appointment.

Seems like the Reverend's a little jumpy, Belle thought as she drove home, intent on talking to Ted Waters.

As she approached her house, she saw a Chelsea police squad car in her drive. *Oh, no. What now?* she thought as she pulled into her driveway. She got out and walked toward an officer standing by the car. "What's going on?" Belle asked, not a bit happy that the neighbors had more grist for the gossip mill.

"Your neighbor called to report a breaking and entering. Your husband wasn't home, so we came right over. Your back door is broken in, so you'll need to let us know if anything was stolen."

"Did my neighbor see the person responsible?" Belle asked.

"She gave a vague description: we think they were two high school kids."

"This is just great—something else to worry about," Belle replied, shaking her head.

"We've dusted for fingerprints. The ground is pretty dry, so we didn't get any footprints. Since we probably won't find much evidence, we'll have to file the report and wait until another similar crime is committed. Then we might find out who broke into your home."

"Thanks for coming over," Belle said sincerely. "Do you want me to go in the front or the back door?"

"As far as we know, they didn't approach the front door."

"Then I'll go in the front and look around."

"You might consider getting yourself a dog for Mother's Day, Mrs. Franklin."

"We just might do that."

Belle looked throughout the house and concluded that the thieves were looking for money. The only thing missing was some cash that sat in an empty jar on the kitchen counter. But she noticed that all the keys were gone from a key caddy on the wall by the back door.

Mrs. Mitchell, the neighbor who called the police, stopped in to explain her actions and to get Belle's blessing for acting as she did.

"The thieves were here less than a minute, Belle. I saw them go around the back of the house, and then I heard loud noises. When I went outside, I saw that they had broken in, so I called 911. Within seconds, I heard the sirens and the two men took off running."

"Thank you. I am most thankful for your quick action. You're a good neighbor," Belle said, assuring her friend that she approved of her calling the police.

♬ ♪ ♬ ♪ ♬

Barb Sousa, the Teen Youth Leader of Living Waters Church approached Belle. "Mrs. Franklin, we know you had nothing to do with Mr. Spencer's death. We know you are investigating it, not only to prove your innocence, but to explain how he died. The kids and I have been wondering how we can help. Can you think of anything?"

Belle hesitated a few seconds, "Yes, as a matter of fact, I can."

"Before you tell me, you do realize however we help, we can't put the young people in harm's way."

"Absolutely. But I'm actually thinking about how they could honor Mr. Spencer, rather than helping with the investigation."

"Please explain."

"Might the teen group come up with a way to pay tribute to Roland, emphasizing his gift of music?"

"Certainly! That's a wonderful idea, Belle."

"I have a few thoughts, but I don't want to interfere with their creativity," Belle said.

"Could you maybe meet with them and explain what you are doing as a detective? Then you can suggest ways to honor Mr. Spencer."

"Sounds good. When can we do this?" Belle asked, getting her calendar out of her purse.

"Well, we meet today after school in the church youth room. Is that too soon for you ?"

"Not at all. The sooner the better. There's no time to waste."

"Great. Could you be there about three-thirty?"

"Certainly. I'll see you then."

♫ ♪ ♫ ♪ ♫

Since Belle had a few minutes, she called Lou to bring him up to speed.

"One of the three chemists in the old photo, Blake Schooley, died in a laboratory explosion at the University of Wisconsin.

Roland, of course, is dead, and the third man is Ted Waters, who works at Dow Chemical in Midland."

"Interesting. Great work, Belle!"

"I tried to call Dr. Waters, but his voice mail said he's at a conference in California and wouldn't be reachable."

"Well, the fact is that anyone can be reached, anytime, anywhere," Lou replied. "Technological advances have made incommunicado a thing of the past. I'd guess he's not really in California, but he needs an excuse not to talk with you."

"Why should I doubt him, Lou?"

"Because that's the job of a detective—always doubt, always question. Especially if something doesn't seem right or logical, like a business person being inaccessible."

"I see."

"Call Dow Chemical in Midland and ask to speak to him. If you get the same voice mail, ask to speak to his supervisor to learn how to reach him in California. I'll wager the supervisor will say he knows nothing about a conference, and that Waters is in Midland."

"Okay. I'll do that. What would he have to hide, Lou?"

"Don't know. Maybe nothing."

"I'm also becoming suspicious of Reverend Norris."

"Now you're catching on!" Lou chuckled.

"To what?" Belle asked confused.

"The last time we talked, you were adamant that Reverend Norris would be above all of this. Now you are challenging your own thinking. Great work! As I said, you need to doubt and question. You'll be another Jessica Fletcher before you know it!"

"Well, nothing major has come of it yet, but I'm watching body language, tone of voice, attitude. I think I should pay just as much attention to these cues as the words that come from someone's mouth. Maybe more."

"You're right!"

"My next update is that our home was recently broken into by a couple of kids. They got some money from the kitchen, but then took off when they heard the police sirens. We need to repair the back door, get some good locks and maybe a big watchdog, and we'll be back in business."

"I'm sorry to hear that, Belle. Do you think this is related to your investigation?"

"Oh, I'm sure it is not."

"Whoa. Not so fast. There is a reason behind every action. Somebody may want to scare you off the case or sabotage your investigation by stealing your computer."

"I see your point. I'll see if it's part of a pattern, but I'm pretty sure it is a B and E with no connection to the investigation."

"The invasion of one's property is very upsetting," Lou said, sympathetically. "I hope the boys are caught."

"Thanks. I hope so, too. In other news, our church youth group wants to help with a memorial to Roland."

"Great. And, in another abrupt change of subject, what did the doctor say about Roland's prescription that wasn't filled?" Lou asked.

"It was for epinephrine, which is given for anaphylaxis."

"Was it prescribed by his own physician?" Lou asked.

"I don't know."

"There's another lesson, Belle. When a detective says, 'I don't know', it means, 'Find out!'"

"Sorry, Lou."

"No apologies needed, Belle, but next time remember; a mental 'I don't know' should trigger an urge to find out."

"Got it. That's news from Chelsea, Lou. Just wanted to let you know what's going on."

♫ ♪ ♫ ♪ ♫

That afternoon, Belle met with the teens in the youth group. She explained in general what she was doing to try and solve the mystery of Mr. Spencer's death in the choir loft, and of her wish to have Roland honored. "I would like you to help me and the choir by finding a way to remember Roland."

One of the girls who had been listening intently politely raised her hand.

"You have a question, Rhoda?" Belle asked.

"Not a question, but a comment. I don't think anyone killed Mr. Spencer."

"That's a fair conclusion. Many others think that, too," Belle admitted. "But, I'm not sure at this point. Why don't you think it was murder?"

"There's just no logical reason for anyone to kill him," Rhoda began. "I can't think of any reason a sane person would want to go to prison for life. You wouldn't, Mrs. Franklin; no member of the choir would; Reverend Norris wouldn't. I mean, I see no motivation to kill."

The silence indicated those in the room couldn't counter Rhoda's observation.

"Thanks, Rhoda," Belle said sincerely. "Good thinking."

"Thank you. But I really like your suggestion to help keep his memory alive."

"I appreciate your kind comment."

Gwen Rubach spoke up next. "I represent the other side of the coin."

"The other side of what coin?" Belle asked, unsure of what Gwen meant.

"I disagree with Rhoda. I think Mr. Spencer was murdered, and I think it has something to do with his history. There may be motivation to kill there."

"How do you mean, Gwen?" Belle asked.

"Revenge is at the heart of most personal conflicts."

"Why would a friend kill a friend?" Belle asked.

"Because he was crazy."

"Okay, Gwen. Thank you," Belle replied. "There you have it: two vastly opposing viewpoints."

After several more minutes of discussion, the youth leader brought the meeting to a close. "We thank you, Mrs. Franklin, for giving us an opportunity to honor Mr. Spencer. Let's give Mrs. Franklin a warm round of applause."

"Thank you. If you need money to implement your idea, just let me know. I am sure the choir will contribute. I can't wait to hear your plans!"

♫ ♪ ♫ ♪ ♫

Driving home, Belle gave some thought to Gwen's notion. Could Ted have murdered Roland? Belle called Lou.

When Belle finished explaining the situation, Lou replied, "What does the police report look like for Blake's death?"

"I haven't a clue," Belle admitted.

"Get that report," Lou said.

"Will the campus police give it to me?" Belle asked.

"You won't know until you ask."

"Right. I'll let you know what I find."

Belle decided not to bother with phone calls and e-mails. She told Hank she'd be gone for a couple of days and to call her if anything important came up.

Belle literally threw some clean clothes into a suitcase, gathered some personal items, and was soon on I-94 heading for Wisconsin. At a rest stop, Belle called Tom Everlast, who agreed to lead choir practice.

Six hours later she pulled into a visitor's parking spot outside Campus Security at the University of Wisconsin in Madison. Inside the building she asked to speak to an on-duty officer.

Belle was introduced to officer Stacy Bastian, who invited her into a conference room where Belle explained her goal.

Stacy listened, then leaned toward Belle. "Okay, let's get one thing settled before we even get past 'Hello', she said firmly. "Are you a Michigan State or U of M fan?"

"Go Blue! Shall I sing a verse of 'The Victors?'" Belle asked with a grin.

"Don't you dare let a Michigan fight song bounce off the walls of this building, Mrs. Franklin!"

Belle smiled and said, "I like you already. You've made me feel welcome after a long ride."

"Okay. Now, how can we help a friend from Michigan?" Stacy asked.

"A man died in my choir loft. It might have been natural, or it might have been murder, or maybe something in between. I'm an amateur detective—I probably shouldn't even use that term, since I have no credentials. But I've been rumored to be the murderer, so I've made it my business to find out how the man died."

"Interesting. Good for you for getting involved."

"I figure it can't hurt, and I'm getting good mentoring from Lou Searing, a Michigan private eye."

"Okay, your following up must have something to do with the University of Wisconsin. How can we help you?"

"A chemist named Blake Schooley was killed in a laboratory explosion here in Madison. I'd like to find out as much as I can about this accident, which perhaps wasn't an accident."

"You're in luck—I'm familiar with that incident. I wasn't lead investigator, nor the report-writer, but I was involved with the emergency procedures. Would you like to see our file?"

"That'd be great."

"Let me find you coffee and a quiet place so you can read the report without distractions."

"Coffee would be great. I was raised on a farm, up early feeding the animals, and came to rely on Mr. Caffeine to get me through my morning chores. And, a small room to read would be perfect."

"Coming up," Stacy replied as she left the conference room to get coffee.

Belle was expecting a file folder several inches thick, so she was surprised when Stacy handed her a rather thin collection of documents. Sitting alone in a bare break room, steam rising from her coffee, she opened the folder and began to read.

CAMPUS EVENT #127

AUGUST 12, 2010

CHEMISTRY HALL, LABORATORY B

VICTIM: Dr. Blake Schooley. Full Chemistry Professor, age 49.

SUMMARY: An explosion occurred at 8:16 p.m. Dr. Schooley was alone in the lab working on an experiment (source: Dr. Bonet).

A combination of ammonia and hydrogen peroxide heated beyond the boiling point is believed to have caused the explosion that killed Dr. Schooley instantly. There appear to have been no outside factors in the explosion. Internal procedures were followed re: evacuation, shutting down of machines, and securing cabinets containing flammable materials.

Another page was a summary of the autopsy and certificate of death. The cause of death was reported as, "asphyxiation due to lack of oxygen."

Belle wasn't satisfied with such a nondescript explanation. She wanted to know what research Blake was involved in and why he would have mixed these particular chemicals to such an extreme temperature. While no other cause of death was noted, what looked like an accident may have had a deeper cause.

Where were Roland and Ted when the accident happened? Belle wondered. She had the facts in the event on campus, but apparently no one looked further to understand what might have been behind the accident.

Belle thanked Security Officer Bastian for her kindness and help, then asked, "Where is the chemistry building on campus?"

"Actually, I'm headed in that direction. I can take you there."

"Thank you."

As the two rode in the campus security vehicle, Stacey asked, "The accident report left some questions, I take it?"

"Yes. I can't imagine that a chemist with Blake's level of education and experience would ever misuse a Bunsen burner with a volatile mixture. Unless it was a suicide, that's far outside the norm."

"I agree. To be honest, I suspected it was a staged accident, but it wasn't my place to comment," Officer Bastian replied. "I'm not a CSI, not even a detective, for that matter. But, the report begs the question, 'How could an experienced chemist have allowed those chemicals to reach a temperature such that an explosion was likely?'"

The car pulled up to the chemistry building, and Belle once again thanked her escort. She entered the building and told the receptionist she wanted to speak with either the Department Head or a faculty member who had known Blake Schooley.

"That would be Dr. Dailey," the receptionist said without a moment's hesitation.

Belle was directed to Dr. Dailey's office, as the receptionist called ahead. The Doctor was waiting at his door for Belle to arrive, and invited her to sit in his office.

"What do you think I can help you with?"

"I understand you knew Blake Schooley," Belle began.

"That's right. We arrived at the University of Wisconsin at the same time, spring of 1987. He had just received his Ph.D. from U of M and I from Notre Dame. Our offices were side by side, and we soon realized we shared an interest in chess. We joined the university chess club and enjoyed hundreds of matches and tournaments. Anyway, you wanted to ask me about his death, I presume?"

"Yes. I read the report of the accident, and I question why Blake would have had the Bunsen burners so high. He certainly must have known that the mixture could explode."

"I thought the same thing." Dr. Dailey nodded.

"Could anyone account for this? Was he alone in the lab prior to the explosion?"

"As I understand it, he was."

"So, can you rule out someone coming into the lab and turning the Bunsen burner up?"

"No, I can't."

"Really?" Belle was surprised.

"People are always walking through, using the lab as a shortcut to get a book, check on an experiment, or confer with a professor. As a prank, someone could have turned the burner up, not knowing the mixture was explosive."

"I see."

"There were rumors circulating that he was murdered, although, in my opinion, it was never confirmed." Dr. Dailey seemed uncomfortable.

"It was never confirmed because...?" Belle asked.

"Because, when the Department conducted its investigation, it was clear that even an undergraduate chemistry student would know an explosion could occur under those circumstances."

"Did the rumors mention a specific person?" Belle asked.

"No, it was just a hunch, held by a faculty member."

"And, who might that be?"

"Me." Dr. Dailey shifted in his chair.

"Did murder really occur to you, beyond the realization that the explosion was inevitable?"

"Blake was not the most popular professor. It was as if he found joy in upsetting students or faculty members. He always had a negative attitude, putting people down. One could almost call him a bully. He was not a likeable guy. I could see through his demeanor, and he knew that I had his number. But he also knew that I had his back."

"So, your theory was not taken seriously?"

"My hunch was noted in the final report to the president of the university, but you're correct, it was never taken seriously."

"Did anyone go to the funeral? The way you describe Blake, I might imagine the funeral home was empty except for you."

"There was a respectable group of mourners. Some family, neighbors, faculty members, and a few out-of-towners."

"Who were the out-of-towners?" Belle asked.

"I think there was a friend from his time at the University of Michigan. Well, I shouldn't say 'I think', rather I should say, 'I know'. We struck up a conversation at the funeral reception. He referred to Blake as one of three men who called themselves 'The Brilliant Chemists'."

"I see. Who was the faculty or family member responsible for sending acknowledgments for flowers and charity donations received in Blake's name?"

"That would be me, as well. I guess I was the only friend Blake had, so the department chair asked me to handle those responsibilities." Dr. Dailey sighed, resigned to the memory.

"Do you have the registration book?" Belle asked.

"I think so. At least, it's probably in a pile here somewhere," Dr. Dailey said, glancing around at several mounds of books and paper cluttering up the office.

"Can I help you locate it?" Belle offered.

"No, please don't touch anything." Dr. Dailey rose, his hand palm out. "I don't mean to be rude, but I know exactly where everything is, and nothing should be disturbed."

"But you just said you didn't know where the book was."

"A challenge! OK, I remember seeing it about two months ago. Therefore it should be on this side of the office. And, it didn't have a high priority, so it would be near the bottom of a pile. As I recall it was a bound book, so that means it should be about here." Dr. Dailey moved some papers around and then held up a blue, oblong, bound book. "Yes! Here it is! You take it. I don't need it any more."

"Thank you. Before I go, could you tell me with who it was you spoke to at the reception—the one who knew Blake from his graduate school days?"

"Oh yes." Professor Dailey opened the book and ran an index finger down the list of names. "I think this is the man," he said, pointing. Belle looked above his fingernail and saw "Dr. Ted Waters."

"And, again, where is he located?"

"Some big company in Michigan, I believe." Perhaps it was Belle's rookie status, but if she had studied the list, she would have also seen Roland's name, as well as Dr. Hartley's.

"Thank you, Dr. Dailey."

"My pleasure. Oh, and let me know what you conclude. I've got a hunch you'll prove me right. Blake was murdered—I'm sure of it."

"I'll keep you posted."

08

Belle headed east on I-94, wishing she could fly home instead of navigating a steady stream of traffic all the way. She stopped to eat around Chesterton, Indiana. After ordering, she called Lou.

"I've spent the day on the University of Wisconsin campus in Madison."

"A very nice campus as I recall, especially at this time of the year. Did you learn anything to move this case along?"

"I think so. A chemistry professor thinks Blake Schooley was murdered. He doesn't think, he's quite certain. Blake was not a popular faculty member, nor was he good with students. He comes across as a faculty bully, so we've several suspects."

"That's okay. Better too many than none at all."

"Also, Ted Waters was at the funeral, so I should be able to find him. Do you want to be in on that interview?"

"Do you want me there, or are you simply inviting me as a courtesy?" Lou asked.

"I want you there. You have the experience questioning witnesses, not me."

"Okay. Just tell me where and when."

"Thanks Lou. I'll get back to you once I find Dr. Waters."

"Before you go. Did the peanuts you found in the group home match those found around Roland's body?"

"That's on the top of my to-do list, Lou."

"If they are the same, that group home worker hops to the top of the suspect list."

"I agree."

♫ ♪ ♫ ♪ ♫

The Living Waters Teen Group discussed several ideas for memorials. Beryl Bishop suggested a garden. Liz Hausserman thought a plaque should be hung in the choir room as a tribute. Tim Sprague suggested planting a tree on the church grounds. Finally, Tony Britton thought a scholarship in Roland's honor given to a deserving musician would be an excellent way to honor Roland.

The group discussed each option, considering the costs and fund-raising opportunities. They envisioned holding a ceremony to unveil the tribute and mulled over a date for the presentation.

Mrs. Stout asked the 43 students at the meeting to vote for their top two ideas. By far, the most popular was to purchase a tree to plant on the church grounds. In addition, they would purchase a small memorial stone acknowledging Mr. Spencer's contributions to the church community. Anyone visiting the memorial would know that he had been valued.

♪ ♪ ♪ ♪ ♪

Belle turned her attention to figuring out how the photo had appeared on the church organ. She dialed Bernard Higgins' phone number; there was no answer, but she left a message: "Please meet me in the choir loft of Living Waters Church this evening at 7:00." She thought this the best way to let him know he was needed without using names or phone numbers.

That evening after dinner, Belle drove to the church and parked a good distance from the building, but in a place where she still had a good view of the doors. She wanted to be able to see anyone who might enter, while not being obvious herself. She also waited to go to the choir loft until after seven, so she would not be surprised by curious strangers.

After watching several people come and go in the church lot, Belle moved the car closer to the building and parked. She walked the short distance to the back door, then made her way to the choir loft, feeling quite certain that nobody was there. But she was wrong: seated in the tenor section were two college-aged young men, patiently waiting as if early for choir practice. She was startled, but recovered quickly.

"You frightened me. I wasn't expecting anyone."

"Bernie said you were looking for him," the first man said. "So, we're here to help you if we can."

"Thanks. And where is Bernie?" Belle asked.

"He said he couldn't be seen in public."

"Who are you two?" Belle asked, puzzled by that answer.

"We're his friends."

"Why would Bernie send you?"

"He told us to ask if you received the photo of the chemists."

"Yes, I did receive it. Is that all?"

"He wants you not to mention the three chemists anymore, for if you do, you might wind up trying to solve his death."

Belle responded surprised. "I've received his message."

"Okay, we'll leave."

"Please tell him I'm sorry for whatever he's going through, and I'll not mention the 'three brilliant chemists'."

"We'll tell him."

"And, what are your names?"

"No need for you to know our names." With that, the two men hurriedly left the choir loft.

♫ ♪ ♫ ♪ ♫

The next day, Belle failed to hear from Ted Waters. She took Lou's advice and called Dow Chemical in Midland.

A pleasant voice answered, "Thank you for calling Dow Chemical. How may I direct your call?"

"I'd like to talk to Ted Waters' supervisor."

"Who is calling?"

"My name is Belle Franklin, and I'm calling from Chelsea, Michigan."

"One moment, please."

After quite a wait, the receptionist came back on the line, "Miss Franklin, I'm afraid Mr. Waters' supervisor isn't available. Can someone else help you?"

"I need to talk to someone who can tell me how to reach Mr. Waters?"

"Oh, I can do that. Mr. Waters is in. I'll ring him for you."

"Thank you." *So much for a conference,* Belle thought.

"This is Ted Waters. How may I help you?"

"Hello, this is Belle Franklin. I'm investigating the death of Roland Spencer."

"Oh, Spence, yeah. But, I can't imagine why you called me."

"Because you're the only living chemist from your group of graduate school friends."

"My gosh, that was so long ago. I don't think I've seen Spence in more than 15 years."

"You were at Blake's funeral. You sat with Roland at the funeral service," Belle replied, proud of having that fact at hand.

"Oh yes, of course. How could I have forgotten that?" Waters sounded chagrined.

"May I talk with you?" Belle asked.

"I'd rather not, Mrs. Franklin. I have a lot on my plate at the moment. I don't think I can find the time."

"Well, we can make this easy or difficult. 'Easy' implies a comfortable talk over coffee or tea. 'Difficult' means I may work with the prosecutor to ask a judge to issue a subpoena and a search warrant so we can confiscate your computer and escort you in for a police interview. So, what will it be?"

There was a pause and then Ted said, "Now that you put it that way, I choose a chat over coffee."

"Wise choice. Tomorrow morning at ten o'clock at the Tim Horton's close to your company."

"I don't think I…"

"I'm calling these shots, Mr. Waters. Ten tomorrow at Tim Horton's. And, if you decide you have another conference in California, the police can find you wherever you are, and it won't be pretty. It might be a good idea to be a little early."

The phone went dead on Waters' end. Belle couldn't believe she had been so assertive. *Hmm, maybe Lou got into my brain for a moment*, she thought.

Belle called Lou to tell him she would see Ted Waters tomorrow at 10, and if he could make it, please come.

While Belle was still talking with Lou, Ted was calling Dr. Handley.

"Guess who's coming to dinner?" Ted asked.

"Sydney Poitier?"

"I wish! I'm meeting with that choir director who thinks she is a detective tomorrow."

"Will she be alone?" Marcia asked.

"I assume so. She didn't speak of bringing anyone along. What am I going to say?"

"Why did you even agree to meet with her?" The professor sounded angry.

"I didn't have a choice."

"Don't be ridiculous!"

"I didn't! She said either I talk to her or be hauled off to jail and my home searched and my computer confiscated. I can't afford that!"

"Listen!" Professor Handley replied sharply. "No one can pin Roland's death on you. If you act like you're trying to hide something, you'll be seen as guilty. Just answer her questions honestly."

"Are you kidding me? You might as well as suggest this woman throw me into a pond with hungry alligators!" Waters was panicking.

"You'll be fine. Let me know how it goes," Handley said mockingly.

"Probably the worst decision of my life was getting to know you," Ted said.

"You won't say that once we get over this minor glitch. I mean, just who is meeting with you?"

"Belle Franklin, a choir director and amateur investigator."

"Oh, PLEASE! A choir director! You send her on a few wild goose chases, and she'll be off your tail for months."

"Well, then give me a goose for her to chase—this isn't a situation I'm comfortable with."

"I'll think about it and get back to you." Handley hung up.

♫ ♪ ♫ ♪ ♫

Tim Sprague, the teen who suggested a tribute to Roland, sat on the organ bench as members came into the choir room for practice. Belle appeared delighted to find Tim in her seat.

"Ah, a new organist. I've been praying for a new one. I guess God chose you."

Tim chuckled. "No way, Mrs. Belle. But you could say he sent me to give you something to think about."

"Tom, can you please take over for a few minutes? Thanks. This way, Tim."

The two went into the music room and sat down. "So, what did God want me to know?" Belle asked.

"I was curious about Mr. Spencer. My uncle is a chemist at UCLA, so I asked him what might give three graduate-school chemists a reason to kill one another."

"Good question!"

"His answer was quick: 'ownership of a patent.'"

"Just like that?" Belle asked.

"Just like that. Can you take it from here, Mrs. Franklin?"

"Yes. Thank you, Tim."

"Good luck, Mrs. Franklin."

♫ ♪ ♫ ♪ ♫

After practice Belle called Lou to inform him of this lead. "A very good tip indeed."

"Do these things come to you right out of the blue, Lou?"

"Rarely, but sometimes."

"This is perfect timing. I'll be able to use this when we see Ted tomorrow."

"Yes, but use it at the right time," Lou advised.

"How will I know the right time?" Belle asked.

"Well, you don't want to start off with 'Have you applied for a patent?' You simply ask questions, and the conversation should move to a point where you can bring up the patent. Go with the flow, Belle. If you miss the moment, I'll interrupt."

"Okay, thanks. See you in the morning."

"Fine. And Belle, I'll expect to hear if the peanuts in the group home match the peanuts found around Roland's body." Lou was fairly certain that Belle had let this go. Belle winced because she had not followed up.

"Of course."

Belle immediately drove to the police station, asked for Chief Purdy, and was welcomed into his office.

"What can I do for you today, Miss Belle?"

"I need to see the peanuts that we found near Roland in the choir loft."

"Have a lead, do you?" Chief Purdy replied.

"I just want to follow up on a possible peanut connection."

"Follow me. We'll go into the evidence room and find the peanuts."

Chief Purdy opened a large plastic bag with a tag that read, "Roland Spencer."

Belle, wearing protective gloves so as not to disturb the evidence, reached in, taking two peanuts from the bottom of the bag. She set them on a table and photographed them with her iPhone.

"Do we have a match?" Chief Purdy asked.

"I think so, but I'll need a closer look. Thanks, Chief."

"You're welcome."

♫ ♪ ♫ ♪ ♫

Belle and Lou talked on their cell phones approaching Tim Horton's in Midland deciding to enter the eatery at different times. Belle would go first and find the quietest table. Lou would follow and sit nearby.

"My guess is that Ted may have an attorney with him," Lou said. "If not, he is quite naïve."

"I'm sure he has accomplices. In fact, his phone greeting about that conference in California was probably recorded after someone tipped him off to me. That person could only be Professor Handley."

"Hmm. Now you're thinking like a detective, Belle." Lou grinned, proud of his student. "Anyway, don't be surprised if he comes in with someone."

"If I were him, I would certainly want another set of ears listening, whether that be a wife, friend, colleague, attorney, or accomplice," Belle explained. "My gut says that Ted is a brilliant chemist, but not a hardened criminal. He won't be alone."

Because of her solid prediction, Belle was surprised to see Ted sitting alone. She recognized him from the photo of the three men, so she greeted him.

"Mr. Waters?"

"Yes. Mrs. Franklin, I presume," Ted said, rising.

"Thanks for agreeing to see me this morning," Belle replied. "I'm going to get a cup of coffee. Can I get you anything?"

"No, thank you."

When Belle returned, Lou had entered and taken a seat at the table next to them. No one appeared to be with Ted. *This is odd,* Lou thought.

"What did you want to ask me?" Ted began.

"As you may have heard, your friend, Roland Spencer, died in the choir loft of my church. As choir director, I was the last to see Roland alive so I am a suspect. I live in a small town, and some folks are convinced I'm a murderer. To save my reputation and solve the murder, if there was one, I am investigating the circumstances surrounding his death."

"Am I a suspect, too?" Ted asked.

"I wouldn't use the word, 'suspect'. But you're a person of interest, in that you were a friend of his in graduate school. You might have information that could help me explain how Roland died."

"I see."

"Did you kill Roland?" Belle asked. Lou winced and almost coughed on his donut. *Boy, she wastes no time getting to the point,* Lou thought.

"I think I had a role in it, yes." Lou could hardly believe what he had heard.

"How do you mean?" Belle countered.

"Well, the three brilliant chemists, as we were known back then, loved to experiment. We enjoyed coming up with way-out ideas and we wanted to discover a combination of chemicals that would cause an ideal to become real."

"Did this happen?" Belle led on.

"I think so. The three of us created a formula that would stop the growth of sod at two inches while allowing the grass to remain healthy."

"Why would you want to do that?" Belle asked.

"The obvious reason was to be leaders in the 'green' movement, which was not even on the radar screen back then."

"I see. Sounds like a miracle concoction."

"Exactly. You can imagine lawn care businesses would be affected. But, our invention never made it to the market. Lobbyists from every part of the lawn service industry worked to see that our chemical never became available."

"I assume you three have a patent on this?" Belle asked.

After a telling pause, Ted answered. "That has been an open sore for years. We weren't aware at first, but Roland worked with a patent attorney to make sure he, and he alone, had patent rights to the formula."

"I see," Belle continued. "I don't know much about patents, but I think that means that any money earned from the sale of such a product would go to Roland only. Or, if the rights to the formula were sold to a chemical company, only he would get the money."

"That's precisely what it means, Mrs. Franklin. I'm sure you can imagine how Blake and I felt, being cut out of the monetary benefit, since we all contributed to the product."

"I would be pretty upset. No, I would be mad, big-time," Belle replied.

"We were. But when we confronted him, Roland simply shrugged it off, implying that we never had any agreement to apply together."

"And your response?"

"Well, at first we turned a cold shoulder. Then Blake and I talked to an attorney who told us we had no case. She said it would be next to impossible to convince a judge or jury that Roland acted criminally. We could prove he acted unethically, but proving anything illegal would be impossible, and she wouldn't take the case."

"Thanks for the explanation. Where did this happen?" Belle asked.

"We were in the doctoral program at the University of Michigan. We were called Fellows, recipients of prestigious scholarships. When the three of us first met, the rapport between us was electric. We had so much in common, our strengths helped one another. We were interested in experimenting, research, and problem-solving with undergraduates."

"In other words, you three hit it off."

"Exactly."

"Did you three have the same advisor?" Belle asked.

"Yes. Dr. Handley."

"Did you teach undergraduate classes?"

"No, most doctoral students do that, but our fellowship was research-based. Our job was to make major discoveries in the health field, like find a cure for cancer, further genetic research, find a prevention for diabetes or Parkinson's. Our time was not spent in the classroom, but in the lab, which was practically our home. On some days, we were there continuously, monitoring experiments, collecting data, discussing our findings with colleagues. In fact, each of us had his own laboratory. We had prestigious status, and we faced huge expectations to succeed. The Ph.D. degree was sort of a token 'thank you'; what we were expected to accomplish made the specifications for a doctoral degree seem like junior high school work."

"And did the three of you accomplish what was expected ?" Belle asked.

"Unfortunately, we didn't. We were dismissed after just two years of a three-year program."

"That must have been difficult. How did that happen?"

"We three sought a patent for a different minor invention, even though we knew the university had rights to patents which were results of work by their students."

"What was this minor invention?" Belle asked.

"We invented a lip balm that will protect lips for weeks at a time. Anyway, we fought that on principle and lost. But, no one told the patent office about the rift and the agency processed the pending patent in our names, finally issuing the patent to the three of us. It wasn't even issued until after we were dismissed, when we were not students in good standing at the university."

"I see. The university wasn't happy about this?"

"They were a lot more than 'not happy'. They became quite aggressive."

"What do you mean by aggressive? Physical, psychological?"

"They threatened to destroy our reputations, to erase our records for the two years we did attend the university; that sort of bullying."

"May I ask a favor of you? A friend of mine, Lou Searing is here helping me investigate this case. Would you mind if he joined us?"

"Fine with me. I've nothing to hide." Belle gestured to Lou who pulled up a chair. Lou and Ted shook hands.

"We were talking about the university not taking kindly to you and your friends being awarded the patent for your chemical invention," Belle reminded Ted.

"That's right."

"So, did you agree to terms?" Belle asked.

"No, we did not. We contacted a patent attorney to see if we had any legitimate claim to the patent. His advice was that the patent was rightfully ours."

"So, you told the University to go fly a kite?" Belle asked.

"A bit more professional than that, but yes, we threw down the gauntlet."

"And, they retaliated?" Belle concluded.

"Definitely. They destroyed all records of our attendance there. They also contacted our employers at the time and tried to ruin our careers."

Lou chose to enter the conversation, "Mr. Waters, I guess I don't understand why this is a big issue. You admitted that your invention was minor, so why does the University care?"

"They care because the invention, when refined, could be highly practical."

"Why?" Lou asked. "What am I missing here?"

"They believed if they had the patent, they could tweak the formula and develop unlimited applications. For example, medication for cold sores that disappear in a couple of hours."

"I see. So, if the university has the patent, it could be worth millions in various forms, and a whole host of people want this formula. Consequently, if you have the patent, you could make millions, if not billions."

"That's right," Ted sighed.

Belle changed the subject. "Why did you try to avoid me when I first wanted to talk to you?"

"I thought you were one of the university attorneys trying to make my life difficult."

"Now, you find out I'm an investigator trying to solve the death of one of your colleagues."

"Right."

Lou asked, "Why did Blake Schooley die?"

"That's puzzling. I haven't a clue," Ted replied. "He should never have made a mistake like that, but apparently he heated something to the explosion point."

"I didn't ask *how* he died. I asked *why* he died," Lou clarified.

There was a telling pause. Suddenly Ted's demeanor changed from calm and willing to talk to decidedly agitated.

"How should I know? The man lived in Wisconsin. I hadn't been in touch with him in years!"

Lou continued. "Do you know Bernard Higgins?"

Ted rose. "This meeting is over. I need to get back to work." Without a farewell, Ted walked out of Tim Horton's, got in his car, and drove away.

"You touched a nerve, Lou," Belle said.

"The man was telling you lies," Lou said.

Belle was shocked. "How could you tell? His answers sounded fine to me."

"He was on a roll."

"What did I miss?" asked Belle, dejectedly.

"I guess I owe you an apology, Belle."

"Okay, but why?"

"If I planned to drive all the way to Midland for a day of my life on the road, I wanted to find out who the man is. So, I asked Jack Kelly to check his background."

"I thought Jack was in Mexico," Belle replied. "What did he find?"

"Jack is in Mexico. The technology is such that he can get information from anywhere in the world. When Jack entered Ted's name in the search engine, one post was especially telling. It was a photo of the three chemists along with a headline, 'Chemistry friends from graduate school combine for 13 under par to take the 2009 Madison Open for Scientists.' Jack then contacted the University of Michigan alumni office, and while they wouldn't give out personal information, they did confirm that the three chemists are dues-paying alumni."

"So, being disowned by the U of M and his not seeing Blake for a number of years were bogus," Belle concluded.

"Good lies."

"A wasted meeting?" Belle asked.

"An excellent meeting! Anytime you get facts or lies, the meeting is worthwhile. The question is, why does Ted need to lie?" Lou asked.

"Because the truth would in some way shame the liar."

"Good," Lou replied. "Carry your reasoning a step further."

"He killed Blake and Roland?" Belle asked.

"Could be, but you may be jumping too far ahead. For now, let's just say he doesn't want us to know—and here, you fill in the blank, with the opposite of the lie."

"He had interacted with Blake, and he graduated in good standing from the University of Michigan."

"Yes, and anything beyond that is conjecture on our part. But we can ask why he doesn't want us to know he and Blake were together before Blake died in that explosion."

"And all the talk about a patent?" Belle asked.

"You've more footwork to do now. Your next stop is the federal government patent office in Detroit. See if our chemists or the U of M own patents involving research findings for a spray to curtail grass growth or for a lip balm formula."

"Thanks for coming all the way over here just for this short interview. It seems hardly worth your while, Lou."

"I have a good friend, Harry Grether, who lives in Midland. We're going to catch up on each other's lives at lunch. Harry is a writer, motivational speaker, and a good friend, and seeing him makes the trip worthwhile. Helping you is icing on the cake."

"This Ted character is becoming quite a person of interest. I'll get on his tail and see where it takes me."

"Always a joy to see you, Belle."

"Thanks, Lou."

"Oh, you were going to tell me how the peanuts from the group home compared to the ones found near Roland's body."

"The two sources of peanuts are identical," Belle replied.

"And, what does that tell you, Belle?"

"It tells me I need to talk to the group home lady."

"Yes. That is the most substantial clue to date. Please follow up on it as soon as possible, Belle—this could break the case," Lou replied, energized by the discovery.

♫ ♪ ♫ ♪ ♫

Driving west, Lou focused his attention on Belle's case. Usually he conferred with Jack because two heads were always better than one. But Jack was unavailable, and Lou was ready to give serious thought to this case.

His summary of facts were as follows: Roland is dead, Blake is dead. Ted is a liar. No cause of death can be determined for Roland. An explosion in a lab killed Blake. Roland had allergy issues. The chemists may have invented a means to curtail lawn growth. Bernard Higgins is missing, or at least unreachable. A patent, or a challenge to a patent may be ongoing. Lou pulled into a rest area in order to jot down these ideas, lest they escape his consciousness.

Based on his thoughts, Lou was concerned that Ted had either been involved with the deaths of Blake and Roland or, if he hadn't, he might be next to die. In Midland, Ted hadn't seemed fearful. At this point, Lou decided to rule out anyone in Living Waters Church as a subject and concentrate his energy, and/or advice to Belle, on Ted Waters.

09

When a receptionist answered the phone in the patent office in Detroit, Belle asked, "May I speak to a patent attorney or someone familiar with basic patent information?"

"One moment, please."

Almost immediately she heard, "Esther Grimes. How can I help you?"

"Miss Grimes, I'm Belle Franklin, from Chelsea."

"That's my home town! Is that little place still on the map?" Esther asked.

"Oh yes—prospering, as a matter of fact."

"I used to go to the Living Waters Church there as a teen," Esther remarked.

"Oh my goodness. I'm the choir director and organist there."

"Mrs. Franklin?"

"That's me."

"I hardly believe it! I was in your youth choir about 10 years ago. A skinny girl with glasses who usually sang off-key. At least you always seemed to scowl while looking at me."

"I'm sorry, Esther. I'm sure my mind was deep into the music and not on a member failing to nail the required pitch."

"You helped me appreciate music. Now, how can I help you?" Esther replied.

"Do you remember Roland Spencer—a large man with a beautiful bass voice?"

"I think so. I went to church whenever I was home and I didn't know him, but I knew of him."

"Well, Roland died in the choir loft after practice a few weeks ago. It hasn't been determined yet whether his death was murder."

"How awful! But I don't understand what that has to do with the patent office," Esther remarked.

"Let me explain. I have an interest in solving Roland's death, because I am a suspect in the minds of the public. I may have been the last to see him alive."

"Mrs. Franklin, if you ever need a character witness, I would be happy to vouch for you. I doubt you could put a mousetrap in your garage."

"Thank you, Esther. That's very kind." Belle took a deep breath before continuing. "When Roland was at the University of Michigan in the chemistry doctoral program, he and some friends developed a product that, when put on sod, could curtail growth at two inches."

"Okay, possible, I suppose."

"I think they may have sought a patent, or maybe one was issued, to either these men or to the University of Michigan. If it was issued, I want to know whether the patent stipulates who has rights to the product in the event of the death of the three principals."

"I can put those specifics into my computer and have the answer to your questions very shortly."

"That would be great. What information do you need from me?" Belle asked.

"The names of the three chemists, and a short description of the invention."

"Okay, the three are Blake Schooley, Roland Spencer, and Ted Waters. Also, the University of Michigan could have sought the patent themselves, or maybe they are a part of this group. The short description might be something like: A formulation that, when applied to a lawn, will curtail growth at two inches, while the grass remains green."

"I'm putting the specs into our database. And, presto, the pertinent information is on my screen: The patent number is 98759973, issued to Roland Spencer."

"Does the application state who obtains the rights after a death?" Belle asked.

"Beneficiary is the Holy Living Waters Church. How about that? Wait a minute, I see an asterisk. Apparently, the patent was contested by a Dr. Waters of Midland and a Dr. Handley of Ann Arbor."

"So, if the judge rules in favor of the University, U of M gets the rights to the patent and not our church. Am I right?"

"Yes, you are correct, and the University of Michigan would be the big winner if Ted were to die."

"Esther, can I get a copy of the patent?"

"Sorry, Mrs. Franklin, we can't release a copy without a court order."

"I may need that eventually, but you have been extremely helpful. Thank you."

"The pleasure's been mine. Give Chelsea my best regards."

♫ ♪ ♫ ♪ ♫

Belle called Professor Marcia Handley and invited her to join her for lunch the following day.

"May I ask why I'm offered the pleasure of your company?" Dr. Handley asked.

"I wanted to thank you for pointing me to Dr. Waters," Belle replied. "I've had a chance to talk with him, and he was most accommodating."

"I thought he might be helpful. Yes, I can meet you for lunch tomorrow. How about noon at Starbucks in downtown Ann Arbor?"

"That sounds great. I trust you'll recognize me from our previous meeting?"

"Yes, I'll recognize you. See you tomorrow at noon," Marcia said, ending the call.

♫ ♪ ♫ ♪ ♫

Belle was not familiar with downtown Ann Arbor, so she used her GPS. Finding Starbucks could not have been easier; the GPS brought her right to the front door.

The two women shook hands and slid into a booth.

"I have a faculty meeting at 12:30 so I'm not going to order. What do you need from me?"

"As I said, I simply wanted to thank you for helping me a week ago."

"You're very kind, but I'd guess you have something else on your mind."

"Yes, I do."

"Please tell me, so I can be on time for my meeting."

"Okay. I'm curious to know why you called Ted Waters after our last visit."

"How do you know I called him?" Marcia countered, surprised at Belle's comment.

"Because shortly after I left, I called him too. His answering machine had a false message about a conference in California. How else could he have been warned to disappear if you hadn't alerted him?"

"I did call, but not for the reason you think. I let him know we had visited and you wanted to see him. But the phone message was not my idea."

"Why did you feel compelled to talk to him?"

Professor Handley appeared to be looking for an acceptable and logical reason for her call to Dr. Waters. Finally she blurted out, "Well, wouldn't you?"

"Wouldn't I what?" Belle asked.

"Call someone if a murder investigator planned to pay him a visit? I'd want someone to call me."

"Ted is quite the liar. Was that character trait obvious when he was a student?"

"No. That would be totally out of character for Ted."

"Well, I know you will call Ted at your earliest convenience. Dr. Waters is a suspect in Roland's death, as well as Blake's death in Wisconsin."

"Sure doesn't sound like the Ted I know."

"Well, it's the Ted I know, and nothing sends up more red flags than lying to an investigator. He could have held up a sign that read, 'I did it!'"

"Ted is a complicated character. As you investigate, you may find inconsistencies, and—well, let's just say he's not an easy man to understand. He's brilliant beyond words, but understanding him takes some doing. That's probably why he never married; he's a most eccentric person."

"Is he capable of murder?" Belle asked.

"I suppose everyone is capable."

"I suspect Blake and Roland were unmarried also. Correct?" Belle asked.

"It wouldn't surprise me. They are, or were, married to chemistry and other passions."

"Was it a love triangle?"

"My gosh, no. Those guys are straight arrows." Professor Handley glanced at her watch. "Listen, I've got to get going," she said, reaching for her spring wrap.

"I understand, but before you leave, does anyone else know him well?"

"I have no idea. I really must go."

"Thanks for meeting me, Professor Handley."

Belle remained in the booth, thinking. *Maybe I'm giving too much attention to this patent business. Maybe Ted isn't the* person of interest I thought. Maybe something else is going on here. And, is someone holding Bernie hostage?

♫ ♪ ♫ ♪ ♫

Belle drove to the group home to drop off her fifty-dollar payment, hoping to interview Megan. "Do you have a few minutes for me?" Belle asked.

"Sure do."

"As you know, I'm investigating Roland's mysterious death."

"Yes. How's that coming?"

"So far I'm just gathering a lot of information and talking with several people."

"I'm sure you'll figure it out."

"How is Aria doing in her new home?" Belle asked.

"It's an adjustment to go from living with one person to a house-full of companions. But she revels in the attention."

"That's good. Here's my weekend check for Dick's work."

"Thank you. I'll see that he gets this."

"A few questions, if I may?"

"Certainly."

"The peanuts in the big bowl in the living room seem to be the exact same kind as those found around Roland's body. Naturally I'm curious if they are."

"I sure didn't kill him, if that's where you're going."

"I'm only going for facts. Was it possible that Dick dropped some peanuts in the choir loft on one of his walks with Aria?"

"Certainly is, but it didn't happen," Megan replied quickly.

"Dick knew you were angry with Roland, didn't he?"

"Yes. It was common knowledge."

"Dick would want to please you, and one way would be to punish Roland for making you angry by failing to pay him for his dog-care chores."

"I can see where you're coming from, Mrs. Franklin, but it didn't happen."

"Are you with Dick 24/7?" Belle asked.

"No, most of the men who live here are free to leave at will."

"So, he could have taken some peanuts to the church and spread them around where Roland sits in the loft?"

"Let me shorten your suspect list. I didn't even know Roland sang in a choir, let alone what church he went to. Nor would Dick have any idea where Roland spends his time."

"Is Dick here?"

"No, he's at the YMCA—swimming day."

"I'd like to talk to him within the next day or two."

"I'll tell him when he gets home. Should he call you, or will you call him?"

"Here's my card; please ask him to call me."

♫ ♪ ♫ ♪ ♫

Belle felt a wave of guilt over not acting immediately on her suspicion that Bernie was being held against his will. While she expected he was alive, she believed that any intervention could endanger his life. On the other hand, why would the two men meet her? The last time she had contacted Bernie was when she left a voice message on his phone. She called Lou.

"I need some advice," Belle began. "I've seen on television detective shows that the technology exists to trace the location of a cell phone. I think Bernie has his phone with him, or if not, someone may be monitoring it. Does this technology really exist? If it does, how can I use it?"

"Let me call the FBI in Detroit," Lou suggested. "They do have the technology and would most likely be willing to use it, but the request to do so would need to come from the Chelsea Police Department."

"Great. I'm concerned about Bernie. He tried to help me but may be held hostage."

"I'll get back to you soon."

"Thanks, Lou."

♫ ♪ ♫ ♪ ♫

Ted Waters called Professor Handley. "I'm toast."

"What do you mean?"

"They've got my number. That Searing guy knew I was lying. I'm sure he thinks I'm the one they need to trap."

"As I've said before, no investigator can find evidence to convince a jury that you were involved in any way with either Roland's or Blake's death. Trust me."

"I'm not good at deception. I don't understand the crime world. It's only a matter of days before I'm trapped." Ted was so nervous, he had trouble speaking.

"Ted, pull yourself together! This will blow over soon."

"I don't think so. I'm done."

"Ted, you are not!"

"You can't go up against Lou Searing and win. He's helping that choir director, so there are two minds after me."

"Ted, how can I put your mind at ease?"

"I'm leaving Midland. I didn't expect to, but I'm leaving while I still have some freedom."

"Where are you going?"

"I'm not sure, but it will be far away."

"Ted, listen, why don't you…" The phone went dead. "Ted? Ted!"

♫ ♪ ♫ ♪ ♫

Ted immediately prepared to leave. He took what money he could find and drove to Indian River to where his cottage was on the Pigeon River. Once settled in, he relaxed—the stress was gone. He was safe from the police or anyone working on their behalf.

Professor Handley was beside herself. She knew Ted would probably leave Midland. He was known for making rash and quick decisions, even back in his graduate days. And, with Ted gone, she expected Belle would look to her for an explanation. She was right.

The professor's phone rang, showing Belle Franklin in her Caller ID space. She took a deep breath and answered it.

"Hello, Mrs. Franklin."

"So, you have caller ID?" Belle remarked.

"What do you want now?" Dr. Handley asked, resigned.

"I've learned that Ted has left Midland. Do you know where he went?"

"How would I know?"

"You two seem to communicate well. I'd say you know where he went from."

"I might agree, but Ted and I haven't talked in a while."

"I will stop short of calling you a liar, but I respectfully disagree. You have talked to him, and you know where he is or where he's going." Professor Handley didn't respond.

"Professor, you can keep playing games with me, or you can come clean and explain what's going on. Wild goose chases are not my idea of cooperation."

"I'm not playing a game, Mrs. Franklin."

"The Midland Police said that Ted had stopped by to say he was leaving town, and someone might file a missing persons report. He told the police he had talked to you, so that if anyone felt a need to talk with him, they should contact you, Professor Handley. Now you say you haven't talked to him. Who is the liar—you, Ted, or the police? My bet is on you." There was another pause.

"Okay, yes, he has left. He was intimidated after his last meeting with you."

"Going on the run only deepens my suspicions."

"He knows that, but I don't make his decisions."

"We'll find him, and when we do, the police may not be very understanding," Bell replied coolly.

"He hasn't broken any law. Why would the police care if he leaves town?"

"He's suspected of murder."

"You have no evidence of that, Mrs. Franklin."

"How do you know that? Could it be that you are the evidence?" Belle asked playing the card in her back pocket.

"Me? Give me a break! Nothing could be further from the truth."

"You just lied to me, and I'm supposed to take your word?" Belle's question drew no response.

"You might want to take flight, too, Professor. I can't prove it yet, but in the end you and Ted may be found responsible for the deaths."

"I have a commitment," Dr. Handley said. "You are one crazy and misled woman. You'll never be able to prove that I am Roland's murderer, if he was, in fact, murdered. I had nothing to do with Roland's death!" She disconnected.

10

Lou was assisting the authorities in Marquette County on a case in a copper mine in Michigan's Upper Peninsula. Belle was able to reach him on his cell phone.

"Belle, I'll be in a mine in a minute. Too much going on. I'll call you in a bit."

"OK, thanks."

About two hours later, Lou was back on the line.

"I don't know how miners do it—mining, I mean. I'm not claustrophobic, but a half-hour down in that mine was about all I could handle."

"A mine, that's an odd place to investigate a murder."

"I'll try anything to get to the bottom of a case. What's on your mind?"

"Our Dr. Waters has skipped town. How is that for wearing an 'I am Guilty' sign on his back?"

"That's an assumption on your part, Belle. You must beware of thinking you have it wrapped up. He could skip town for reasons that having nothing to do with your case."

"I realize that, but it seemed clear to me."

"And, you may be right," Lou admitted. "I'm just offering caution."

"I appreciate it, and I stand corrected."

"Anyway, you were saying…"

"Yes, Professor Handley lied to me, and I'm expecting her to take some action. Whether you believe it or not, I think those two are in cahoots, and I think their motivation relates to the patents."

"So, what are you going to do now?" Lou asked.

Belle was embarrassed that she'd let Lou down by obviously forgetting the advice he had given. "I'm a blank, Lou."

"Tracking of cell phone."

"Oh, yes," Belle recalled.

"We'll use the same technology to follow Ted that we'll use to track Bernie."

"Gotcha! I'll learn some day."

"You're doing fine. I don't mean to criticize, but your 'What to do next' answer should have been on the tip of your tongue."

"Thanks, Lou. I am learning."

♫ ♪ ♫ ♪ ♫

Belle hung up, only to have her phone ring again. Her caller ID read, Dick Fox. She pushed the "Talk" button."

"Thank you for calling me, Dick."

"Megan told me to."

"Good. Do you know what an allergy is?" Belle asked.

"Sneeze and blow your nose."

"Yes, that's usually what happens. People can be allergic to a lot of things; pollen, foods, perfumes."

"I have hay fever."

"Exactly. Do you know if Mr. Spencer had an allergy?" Belle asked.

"Peanuts."

"Peanuts? How do you know?" Belle asked, surprised that Dick would know about Roland's allergy.

"He told me once when I picked up Aria for a walk. He said he could die from peanuts."

"Yes, in bad cases, that can happen."

"I know," Dick replied.

"Did you put broken peanuts in the choir loft where Mr. Spencer sat?"

"What does 'loft' mean?"

"A choir loft is where the choir sits in church. It is usually above the people in the pews."

"No, I didn't do that."

"Okay, I needed to ask."

"Miss Megan was very mad at Mr. Spencer. She could have put peanuts in that place."

"I guess that's possible. Thanks for talking with me, Dick. Are you enjoying having Aria in your home?"

"I am happy. Thank you for paying me money."

"You're welcome."

♫ ♪ ♫ ♪ ♫

Reverend Norris was relieved that speculation about Roland Spencer's death was fading. He got an occasional call from the police, but only to confirm or clarify some minor detail.

He found it extremely odd that the police had returned the ice cream container found in the freezer when Roland died. He expected it would be checked for evidence, and finding none, the officers on staff would polish it off for lunch. But, the ice cream was returned without one spoonful taken.

That morning he had skipped breakfast and scheduled a late lunch. He recalled the ice cream still in the freezer—a half-gallon of chocolate chip cookie dough. He took a bowl from the cupboard and dished a couple of huge scoops.

He found some Oreo cookies in the refrigerator, then sat down in the fellowship hall to eat his delightful mid-morning snack. After two delicious bites, he didn't feel well, and he began to sweat profusely. He needed help, but no one was around and he didn't have his cell phone, and he couldn't walk if he had wanted to. When he slid onto the floor, he took out a pen and tried to write on the carpet, but he passed out.

An hour later, Mrs. Sneath went looking for the Reverend when he missed an appointment. "Oh, no!" she bellowed when she saw him sprawled on the floor. She checked his breathing and noted air from his nostrils, but he had a very weak pulse and was unresponsive. She dialed 9-1-1 on her cell phone. The EMS arrived quickly, followed by media, and ambulance-chasers. The fellowship hall was closed off, so reporters waited outside for any word.

That night on the six o'clock news, Belle and most of the rest of Chelsea learned the story: "Reverend Norris, Pastor of the Holy Living Waters Church in Chelsea is hospitalized and is expected to be kept overnight after being found unconscious in the church's Fellowship Hall. He appeared to have been eating ice cream and cookies at the time of his collapse. The incident comes just a week after the death of Roland Spencer in the church's choir loft. The cause of his death is still unknown. More at eleven."

♪ ♪ ♪ ♪ ♪

Belle was relieved that Lou was not in the mine trying to solve his first Upper Peninsula case when she called. "Got it solved, Belle?" Lou asked using his cell.

"Not yet and now there has been another strange happening in my church."

"Did another person die?" Lou asked.

"No, but close. Reverend Norris was found unconscious in the Fellowship Hall. He had been eating ice cream and cookies."

"I assume those foods will be analyzed?"

"I guess so. The police have not talked to me."

"Where were you when this happened?"

"Oh no," Belle moaned. "It hadn't occurred to me..."

"What, Belle?" Lou asked, not making sense of her reaction.

"I was at the church, cataloguing new music and filling the choir members' folders with music for our next concert."

"Sounds like a legit reason to be in there," Lou replied.

"Or it's one more reason to suspect me, Lou. Maybe I should just disappear!"

"Absolutely not! That's what Dr. Waters did, and you know what message that sends. No, stay put, be honest, and gut this out. You'll make sense of it."

"I guess you're right."

"Was there something in the ice cream? Is this the same ice cream noticed when Spencer's death was reported?"

"Yes."

"I've got a friend in Overland Park, Kansas who used to be employed by a dairy, inspecting plants. I'll see what he makes of this coincidence."

"Thanks, Lou."

Lou called Jerry Weiss. "Hi Jerry, Lou Searing here."

"Hi Lou, are the daffodils up in your neck of the woods?"

"They're up, and now we're waiting on the tulips. Carol is hoping to go to the Tulip Festival in Holland this year."

"Hope that works out. What can I do for you?"

"I have a question that takes you back to your dairy days. A man got very sick after eating some ice cream and a couple of Oreo cookies. I'm wondering if there is something that could contaminate the ice cream? I know there are poisons, but I'm looking for something out of the ordinary."

"Could be Salmonella enteritidis."

"Sam-a-what? Slow down and spell it," Lou asked Jerry.

"Sorry. 'Salmon' like the fish, then, 'ella'. The second word is 'enter' and then 'i-tid-is'." Lou scribbled in his notebook.

"Okay, got it. Tell me about this," Lou said.

"In the mid-1990s there was a huge outbreak among people who ate a certain brand of ice cream. It led to a major study involving multiple agencies and departments. They determined that the salmonellosis probably resulted from the contamination of pasteurized ice cream premix. It was transported in tanker trailers that had previously hauled non-pasteurized liquid eggs containing S. enteritidis."

"That would make a person very ill, right?"

"Most definitely. But that was many years ago."

"There hasn't been any mention of a problem in Chelsea, Michigan that we know of," Lou was quick to say. "Could one container have something in it that could kill someone?"

"I'll research it and get back to you."

"Thanks, Jerry."

♫ ♪ ♫ ♪ ♫

Lenore Coscarelli was watching the noon news regarding the Reverend's misfortune. She listened intently: her daughter, Lisa, had had a traumatic near-death experience about a month before. She called the police and then the local hospital to report Lisa's similar results from eating ice cream.

Chief Purdy called Belle.

"I know, I know, you want to talk to me because I was in the church when Reverend Norris became ill. I swear I didn't do it."

"Calm down, Belle, that's not why I'm calling. We just got a call from a woman here whose daughter had a near-fatal experience with ice cream about a month ago. We think there could be some thread winding through Roland's death and now Reverend Norris's illness. We'd like any information you may uncover."

"I'm on it. Thanks for the tip. I'll let you know if and when I learn something."

♫ ♪ ♫ ♪ ♫

A death and a near-death in the Living Waters Church within three weeks. Everybody in town and the surrounding area were talking about events and offering theories about what might have happened.

Rather than run from the confusion, Belle followed Lou's advice and helped the church in Reverend Norris's absence. She arranged for a guest minister to preach on Sunday, reviewed the Reverend's calendar, and made alternate arrangements for commitments or appointments with church members. And, she saw to it that the church's web site was kept current.

She recalled that the police had taken the ice cream as evidence when Roland died. She called Chief Purdy at the police station.

"What did you find out, Belle?"

"First of all, I talked to the nursing supervisor at the hospital and she'll look into the girl's episode with ice cream. Now, about your ice cream."

"Chocolate or vanilla?"

"Does the police chief actually have a sense of humor?" Belle asked with a chuckle.

"It breaks through every once in a while. I'll get serious. What do you need to know?"

"I understand you took a container of ice cream from the freezer at church as evidence when Roland died. Is that true?"

"Yes, we did."

"What did you do with it?"

"We didn't find any problem. We took it back to the church and put it in the freezer."

"Did you analyze the stuff for contaminants?" Belle asked.

"We didn't take a sample because, as far as we knew, the ice cream was safe for consumption."

"Even though Reverend Norris became deathly ill from it?"

"Correct."

"I see," Belle replied, somewhat bewildered by what she had heard.

♫ ♪ ♫ ♪ ♫

Professor Handley was stuck between a rock and a hard place. She overcame her shock and realized that, with police and detectives on the case, she wouldn't get out of this mess. What awaited her was nothing short of disastrous for her career, her department, the university, and her family. There would likely be an arrest, an arraignment, a trial, and then probably years in a women's prison. She would have a life of guilt and embarrassment, estranged from her husband and family. All of this was frightening.

She drove home from the university, pulled the car into the garage, and wrote a note, "I love you. I'm sorry. Please forgive me. Goodbye." She set it on the passenger seat of the car, then pushed the button to lower the garage door. The engine was still running. Within a few minutes she felt light-headed and nauseous, and then she slipped into unconsciousness and died.

Belle learned of Professor Handley's death from an article in the Ann Arbor News. She read:

RESPECTED CHEMISTRY PROFESSOR DIES

Dr. Marcia Handley, 48, of Saline, was found dead in her garage by her son when he arrived home from high school. Professor Handley was discovered slumped over the steering wheel of her car, which was in the garage and still running. Family and colleagues at the University of Michigan are in shock. Authorities allegedly discovered a suicide note, but an autopsy is scheduled to be performed.

Professor Handley was a distinguished chemist, winning numerous awards for her research and teaching. She is best known as the author of a popular high school chemistry text, Understanding Chemistry: A Virtual Tour of the Elements, *which is used in classrooms throughout the English-speaking world.*

Professor Handley leaves behind her spouse, Arnold, a son, Ralph, and a daughter, Ariel. Funeral arrangements are pending at this time.

People are falling like dominoes, Belle thought. *I had better solve this before we get further bad news.* She couldn't help but think of the phrase, "Bad things happen in threes." Roland and Professor Handley were dead and Reverend Norris was in the hospital. Were these three separate events, or were they related?

Belle called Lou to report developments.

"I'm calling to keep you up-to-date, Lou."

"Is it Ted Waters? Are all the brilliant chemists gone?"

"No, but Professor Handley is. I feel somewhat responsible because I talked with her yesterday. I told her that the mystery of Roland's death was proceeding quickly."

"Played your card, huh?" Lou asked.

"It just came out. I think she foresaw the outcome, went home and left her car running in the garage with a suicide note at her side."

"Probably desperation on her part."

"I shouldn't have said what I did. I must have been frustrated by not clearing the case yet. Maybe I scared her to death, pun intended."

"Let me assure you, you are not responsible for her death. We never know what goes on in a person's mind. There may be dozens of reasons for someone to kill themselves, and you shouldn't feel guilty for someone else's actions."

"Well, I'll always feel some guilt."

"Every decision is a choice," counseled Lou. "For reasons unknown to us, she made a choice. But, this is a new direction in your case."

"I guess so. I thought Ted's running away showed guilt. Perhaps suicide is evidence of greater guilt."

"Perhaps, but again, don't jump to conclusions."

♫ ♪ ♫ ♪ ♫

The response to Reverend Norris's near-fatal experience was heart-warming. Many of the local churches sent flowers and cards, and Mrs. Norris kindly greeted everyone who visited her husband in the hospital. She was quite emotional, since her husband had come very close to dying.

Reverend Norris was an advocate for ecumenicalism, one of the community pastors who suggested ways churches could band together for summer worship in the park or community sings at the park band shell. He made suggestions to his peers and led by example by preaching in churches other than his own. He spearheaded youth activities, inviting youth in other churches to participate. After his experience, church members and ministers in the Chelsea area joined together to make sure the Norris family was fed during his hospitalization.

♫ ♪ ♫ ♪ ♫

Ted Waters lay on his cottage bunk trying in vain to rest while constantly worrying about the mess he was in. He felt compelled to pull up an electronic version of the Ann Arbor News to see if there was anything new on the Spencer case. His heartbeat quickened as his eyes fell on the headline, PROFESSOR MARCIA HANDLEY, SUICIDE VICTIM. Deciding he needed to be in Ann Arbor, he packed his few belongings, locked the cabin, and headed south on I-75.

11

One thing Lou Searing did when investigating a murder was to attend the visitation and funeral of the victim, in case he saw or heard something relevant to the case. With that in mind, Belle learned where and when Professor Handley's funeral would be held.

Belle anticipated a large crowd, given that the professor had died fairly young. Colleagues, neighbors, and friends would likely attend, but when she arrived, she discovered only a few cars. Belle parked, went into the funeral home, and approached the sign-in book. She couldn't believe her eyes: written neatly on the third line down was "Bernie Higgins". Relief flooded her; maybe Bernie wasn't in danger after all. Eager to speak with him, she walked into the room with the closed casket, but she didn't see Bernie anywhere. Perhaps he had been at the wake earlier and then left after expressing sympathy to the family.

About an hour later, just as the short ceremony was to begin, Belle spotted Ted Waters—or his twin—out of the corner of her eye. His appearance was disheveled, his clothes wrinkled, and he had not shaved for a couple of days. Ted didn't approach the family but sat in the back, on the end of a row of chairs.

When the brief ceremony was over, he rose and approached Mr. Handley. The two shook hands, and Belle listened from a distance as the husband of the deceased introduced Ted to his two children.

Ted said, "Your wife was a brilliant scholar. She was my mentor while I worked on my degree."

"If I recall, you and a couple other students used to come to the house to discuss theories," Arnold Handley said. "What was it—almost 15 years ago? Weren't the three of you in some kind of fraternity, or perhaps a school club for chemists?"

"There were three of us, but we didn't join anything," Ted replied quietly.

"That's right. You three came up with a chemical that would somehow stop grass from growing, but still stay green."

"That's right."

"Whatever happened to you three?" Mr. Handley asked.

"We graduated and went our separate ways. Blake Schooley went on to the University of Wisconsin; he died a couple of years ago in a lab explosion. Roland Spencer developed health problems and was on a Supplemental Social Security program for some time. He was a wonderful bass and became known for his singing. I am employed by the Dow Chemical Company in Midland."

"I see."

Ted extended his hand, "Well, I'll be going. I'm very sorry for your loss and for the loss of a brilliant scientist."

"Thank you for coming. Dr. Waters, I've wracked my brain. Do you have any idea why Marcia decided to take her life?"

Ted hesitated. "A long time back, Marcia made a conscious decision not to tell her dean of a number of unethical decisions she made. She managed to cover them up, but an investigation into Roland's death would surely bring it all to the surface again. I suppose she couldn't deal with the consequences."

"I see. That doesn't sound like Marcia, but our family wants to know why she died. However, 'unethical' is a word I could never associate with my wife."

"I know, but people will go to extremes to keep skeletons in the closet."

"What did she do?" Arnold asked.

"This isn't the time or place to have this discussion. If you'll wait a few days, I'll tell you what I know, and that may explain her thinking. Can we wait a bit?"

"Yes. Thank you."

Ted nodded with a hint of a smile, then turned and headed for the foyer.

Belle followed after Ted. Catching up with him, she asked, "Dr. Waters, can we talk?"

"I have nothing to say."

"I think you do. In fact I think you want to get this off your chest for your own peace of mind. Am I right?"

Ted stopped. Looking at the carpet he replied, "I suppose you are."

"Sooner or later—probably sooner—the investigation will clarify the confusion that you, your friends, and Dr. Handley created. You realize it's inevitable, don't you?"

"Yes. Our goose is truly cooked. My dad used that phrase when one of us kids could no longer hide something."

"Do you need a ride somewhere?" Belle asked.

"No, I have my car."

"Can we go for coffee before you return to wherever you're hiding out?"

"That's fine," Ted replied.

Sitting in a café, Belle waited for Ted to talk.

"Well, I'll take the goose out of the oven. Maybe I can make the puzzle clear."

"Okay. Will you be truthful this time?" Belle asked

"Yes. There's no more need to keep anything from you."

"Okay, whenever you're ready."

"We were post-graduate student chemists: Blake, Roland, and me. We talked and experimented regularly, and the three of us found Professor Handley open to our ideas. She shared her expertise and even worked some experiments with us. We often included her in our group. Our problems began once we hit on a combination of elements that could stilt the growth of grass."

"I see. Go on," Belle urged Ted.

"Blake was a very jealous person, and he wanted to claim the invention himself. He insisted that he alone was responsible for the spray, a ludicrous claim. He gave it a name, CURB Lawn Spray, and he believed that the rest of us were trying to claim rights to a compound that was truly his." Ted sighed.

"Please continue," Belle said.

"In synthesizing a compound, you need to build the chemical infrastructure by aligning various elements. We all agreed upon the chart that Blake submitted for our review."

"The chart?" Belle asked.

"Yes, the chart describes the elements, the process, and amount of interplay between the elements in a compound."

"Perhaps he should have gotten the full credit."

"Except, that wasn't what we all agreed to. We were in it together, sort of like the three Musketeers: all for one and one for all. All four of us met with a patent attorney who explained how patents work for inventions. He provided the paperwork for us to use. Now, you also should know that the policy of the regents of the university is that any invention created while the principal parties are students or faculty of the university must include the university as a co-signer. As an aside, you would be amazed at the amount of money that comes into the university, any university, that has patents in its name.

"The three of us, in talking to Dr. Handley, decided that we wouldn't include the university as a co-signer of the patent request. We agreed to accept any consequences of this decision, should the university find out and pursue legal action. But Dr. Handley said she would keep this from the university and in so doing assured herself millions of dollars once the compound was marketable."

"This gets a bit complicated, doesn't it?" Belle asked.

"I suppose so, but stay with me."

"I am."

"Okay, now the complicated part. As in an estate plan, you need to declare how the patent will change hands if a signer dies or becomes incapacitated. We agreed that if someone died, the others would remain the beneficiaries. When all of us had died, the beneficiary would be an endowment for scholarships for budding chemists who could not otherwise afford to go to college.

"Professor Handley began to fear that the university would eventually learn about their exclusion from the patent. She then forged all of the documents, so it was clear that the university would not, and could not, be a party to the patent. Dr. Handley also arranged the way the beneficiaries were identified, so that if the three of us were to die, the patent would be hers and hers alone."

"So, did Dr. Handley kill Blake in Wisconsin?" Belle asked.

"I'm going to take the Fifth, Mrs. Franklin, but you are making clear conclusions."

"And if she did kill Blake, did she also kill Roland, or at least arrange for his death?" Belle asked.

"I really don't think so. She knew he wasn't healthy, and she figured he would die a natural death fairly soon. Why get her hands dirty with another murder when she didn't need to?"

"I see. So, you think the professor was planning, in one way or another, to cut the three of you out of the picture. And, with Roland's death, the only thing in the way of her gaining full ownership of the patent was you."

"That's true. But you're only hearing my side of the story. One might logically conclude that I killed Marcia so I would have full ownership of the patent."

"So, did you kill Marcia?"

"No, not in a physical way. I did call and convince her that her scheme would come out as a result of you and Mr. Searing solving Roland's death, though. When we finished talking, she knew it was only a matter of time until she was charged with Blake's murder, along with several major violations of the Board of Regents' policies regarding patents."

"So, she went home and killed herself."

"That appears to be what happened, yes. So, in a sense, I guess I did kill her, but I didn't actually kill her, if you know what I mean."

"So, you now own the patent to the lawn spray."

"Yes, after a lot of legal proceedings I suppose you might say that, but I'm sure the University of Michigan lawyers will intervene. It'll be messy, that's for sure."

"I see. So, let me summarize to be sure I have this straight. Of the four of you, you are the only one living, and the patent for your invention is totally yours. Your conclusion—correct me if I'm wrong—is that Professor Handley saw no reason to kill Roland because he would probably die soon anyway, but that she did kill Blake, and would soon have killed you, too."

"That's what I thought, yes."

"But, why did Professor Handley kill herself?"

"Well, as I said, I convinced her that you and Lou would unveil this conspiracy."

"Meaning that she would be charged with murder."

"Yes."

"And you think Dr. Handley didn't kill Roland because he would die on his own soon enough."

"Yes, but she could have arranged to have him killed and not told me about it."

"Have you any idea how she might arrange his death?"

"I think she'd probably hire the church janitor to kill him."

"Really?"

"It was probably someone in your church."

"That's hard to believe. I know everyone in the church, and no one is capable of murder."

"Think about it. The janitor knows the comings and goings of people in the church. His fingerprints are on everything, as they should be. Janitors don't make much money, and I think she could have come up with some money."

"So, you're saying that Professor Handley hired the janitor to kill Roland."

"No, I said she thought he would die naturally, but if she decided to hurry the death, she could have hired someone in the church to kill Roland. Of the people in your church, the janitor would be a logical person. It could be someone else, or she could have had nothing to do with Roland's death."

"Then who? Is the list long?" Belle asked.

"I don't think so, but I think the tainted ice cream that Reverend Norris ate was meant for you."

"Me?" Belle asked.

"I think you were getting too close to implicating Professor Handley, so she probably asked around and learned that you were the ice cream person. Then she could have set you up to eat the tainted treat."

"Guess I was lucky."

"For sure."

"Our janitor left a week ago because he was so devastated over the two medical episodes in the church. Do you know where he went? He left no forwarding address."

"I haven't a clue."

"I tend to believe your thinking, Ted, but to be honest, it sounds a lot more logical that you're the killer and not Professor Handley."

"Exactly. Professor Handley is brilliant. If she was the killer, I'm sure she planned to make it look like I was the guilty one."

"I still don't see her taking her life," Belle said. "Her plan was on target. She had everything going her way."

"It would appear that way, but something caused her to jump ship and it may have been something unrelated to this case."

The two finished their coffee. As Ted began to rise to pay the bill, Belle said, "So, we're a team from now on? Do you agree? We work together to figure out how Blake, Roland, and Professor Handley died. No more running away, lying about your whereabouts."

"That's the plan," Ted said. "Thanks for listening to all of this craziness. Remember, everything I said are my thoughts on the matter and not facts."

"We'll be in touch."

♫ ♪ ♫ ♪ ♫

While driving home to Chelsea, Belle couldn't get her mind off the possibility of a murderer in her church. Winston was so kind, so sensitive, so devoted to the church. He absolutely would not hurt a fly, and money was not something he coveted. She would see if Mrs. Sneath had a forwarding address for him.

But, if not Winston, then who? She thought of Mrs. Sneath but concluded it totally unlikely. Reverend Norris had a mean streak, which she had witnessed on occasion. Belle quickly came to her senses and dismissed the possibility.

Maybe the killer is a member of the church, Belle thought. But she couldn't imagine who could, or would, do such a thing. She thought of scout leaders, a troubled youth, the women's circle, and the choir. The only logical possibility was someone in the choir, but who?

Lou Searing called to inform Belle he would be coming to Chelsea. He had an idea that he wanted to try out, and depending on what he learned, they might be closer to solving the crime. As soon as Lou arrived in Chelsea, he went straight to the church, parked, and met Belle inside the church doors. Lou was wearing bib overalls and had purchased a bag of peanuts at a store on the edge of town.

"Follow me," Lou said, making his way toward the choir loft. Belle followed, curious as to why Lou wore bib overalls and to what he was thinking. The two walked to where Roland was found.

"What are you doing?" Belle asked. "Please don't keep me in the dark."

"I'm going to put some peanuts in the bib of my overalls and then bend over as if checking a pulse, including bending way forward, so that my head touches the floor. You observe the position of my body when a peanut falls."

"Oh, I see now. Why didn't I think of that?"

"You didn't think of it because, like me, you are trusting of people," Lou replied. "We tend to believe what we are told and we wouldn't want it to be any other way. Can you imagine not believing anything you hear? Not a good way to live."

"Winston claimed the peanuts fell out of his bib when he checked to see if Roland was alive, but you're thinking that no peanuts fell out, or were even in the bib to begin with," Belle considered. "You believe that was simply an excuse because he knew Roland was allergic to peanuts."

"I'm just considering possibilities. I'm not willing to put the janitor in any bad light yet; just testing a theory. Okay, watch for the peanut to fall out of the bib."

Lou leaned over as if checking a pulse or even putting an ear on a chest, but no peanuts fell out. In fact, all the peanuts stayed in the bottom of the bib.

"What does that tell you, Belle?"

"No peanuts fell out, but we don't know if Winston was kneeling or standing," Belle began. "We don't know if the bib material was coarse or smooth. We don't know how jammed full of peanuts it was, or if there were only a few in his overalls. Finally, we don't know if the peanuts were small or large."

"Now you're learning, Belle," Lou said. "You're becoming a great detective."

"Thanks, Lou."

"But, we've learned that Winston's excuse for the peanuts being on the floor next to Roland's body is suspect. We can't take the janitor at his word, can we?"

"No, but we can't arrest him for murder, either."

"That's right. All we have is negative evidence at this point."

Lou stood and looked at his hands. He saw a strand of hair which stuck to his sweaty palm as he knelt down. "Well, what do we have here?" Lou said with some humor.

"Looks like some evidence."

"Has the carpet up here been vacuumed since Roland died?" Lou asked.

"I doubt it. The one who would vacuum said he couldn't set foot up here again."

"So, this strand could belong to Roland or anyone for that matter," Lou concluded.

"It could even be a strand of hair from Megan, the group home worker."

"Bingo!" Lou replied, carefully putting the single strand into a plastic bag.

♫ ♪ ♫ ♪ ♫

The First Methodist Church of Chelsea reached out to help the congregation of Holy Living Waters Church. The minister made arrangements for a sermon each Sunday until Reverend Norris was healthy enough to resume his pastoral duties.

Everything pretty much ran according to schedule thanks to Mrs. Sneath and to Belle.

Belle simply could not understand why an analysis of the ice cream would take so long. She had meant to ask Lou when he was in the church in his bib overalls, but it slipped her mind. She called and was lucky enough to find him at a free moment. "Should it be taking this long to get the lab report on the ice cream we had analyzed?" she asked.

"You've not gotten that yet?" Lou asked, puzzled.

"No."

"I'll call and find out why the delay."

"Thanks, Lou."

Lou dialed the number for Chief Purdy. "What's the holdup on that ice cream analysis?"

"It had to be shipped to the Center for Disease Control in Atlanta. I got a call from the lab director, who said they had to take samples for specific poisons. I think our request went on the back burner."

"Do you mind if I call?" Lou asked.

"Not at all." Chief Purdy gave Lou the name and phone number of the lab supervisor.

Lou called immediately and within a minute was speaking with the lab director.

"I'm calling to inquire about the analysis of some ice cream requested by the Chelsea, Michigan, Police Chief."

"Yes, I talked to him a few days ago and explained the procedures that we require. He didn't ask me to put a 'rush' on it, so I didn't."

"He gave me permission to call you and request that you now prioritize our analysis. We're close to making an arrest in our investigation and need to hear what was in that ice cream. It is important that we know fairly soon."

"I will prioritize it, Mr. Searing."

"Thank you. When might I expect a report?"

"It will be faxed in the morning."

"Thank you very much. Please tell your superior that you deserve a raise."

"It won't do any good, but thank you, sir."

True to his word, a fourteen page report arrived on the tray of Lou's fax machine around 9:45 a.m. the next day. Lou looked at the entire brief, but it read like a dissertation for a doctoral candidate. Lou might as well have been reading Russian. Bottom line, however, was that the ice cream had indeed been poisoned. The flavor was cookie dough, and rodent-killing pellets had been pushed into the ice cream, making it look like the dough or a chocolate chip. The report noted that if help was available, the victim's stomach could be pumped, but without help, death would ensue.

The question was, who put the pellets in the ice cream? Based on the words of Ted Waters, they could have been put there by Professor Handley in an attempt to kill Belle.

Lou sent the report on to Belle. She had to sit down as she read the report because she realized that she could have eaten the ice cream and died. As she finished reading the report, her phone rang. It was Winston. "Hello, Mrs. Franklin. Mrs. Sneath has told me that you want to talk to me."

"Yes, I do. Thank you for calling," Belle began. "I have a few questions."

"Certainly."

"Do you remember the flavor of ice cream that was left in the freezer in the church kitchen?"

"No. It wasn't mine, and I don't like ice cream."

"Do we have rat poison in your supply area?"

"Absolutely not. With all the kids coming in and out of the church, I couldn't risk having rat poison lying around. I haven't seen a mouse in years. The one time I did, I set a trap and had the critter in one night."

"I'm going to come right out and ask you a tough question. Did someone offer you money to kill Roland?"

"Excuse me?"

Belle repeated her question. "Did someone ask you to kill Roland for a large sum of money?"

"Oh my, no. Do people think I killed Mr. Spencer?"

"It is one of many scenarios I'm looking into."

"What's that word mean?"

"Scenario? It means a sequence of events. All I mean is that as I considered a motive for Roland's death, I came across the possibility that maybe you were offered a large sum of money to kill him."

"No, no, no, Mrs. Franklin. Nobody ever talked to me, and even if someone would, I could never kill anyone."

"I know that, Winston, but I had to ask."

"I'm glad you did, so I could set the record straight."

"Have you found yourself another job yet, Winston?" Belle asked. "I miss you and wish you would come back. You were the best maintenance man we ever had. Any chance you might come back?"

"I guess there's always a chance, but the memories are not good. Every time I look at the choir loft, I think of finding Mr. Spencer up there. I'd almost get sick to my stomach."

"I understand. Listen, keep in touch, okay?"

"I will, Mrs. Franklin."

There was no way Belle could conclude that Winston was a killer. If he was, he was the best liar in the whole world. Belle didn't hesitate to scratch his name off her list of suspects.

The other person with a connection to peanuts was Phyllis, and she insisted that she was not a suspect. *There's no sense talking to her*, Belle thought. *She'll just proclaim her innocence as she did before.* The only option she had was to investigate Phyllis without direct contact. With that decided, Belle had a final thought: *Megan from the group home.*

Belle called the police chief in Chelsea and asked for a couple of the peanut shells that were found next to Roland's body. Her wish was granted. She wondered if a peanut was a peanut was a peanut, or if there were different varieties. Would the peanuts Phyllis had in her purse be the same or different from the ones found next to Roland? What about the peanuts from the dish at the group home? She went to her computer and looked up 'Peanuts' in Wikipedia; she found a veritable treatise on peanuts. And, no, there wasn't just one kind of peanut. There were quite a few varieties.

12

As soon as he could do so, Bernie made his way to Belle Franklin. He left a message on her cell phone, then drove to her home and rapped on her front door. Hank answered. "If you're selling something, we're not interested."

"Nope. I'm not selling anything, but I would like to talk to Mrs. Franklin."

"She's here. Come on in."

Hank yelled, "Belle, some fella is here to see you!"

"I'll be right there," Belle replied. She entered their living room where Bernie was seated. "Hi, Bernie."

"I decided to pay you a visit."

"Thank you. I've been worried about you!"

"I want to explain what has been going on."

"I certainly want to know what you have to say."

"I was not kidnapped, nor held against my will. But, I was scared, very scared."

"Scared of what Bernie?" Belle asked.

"After I helped you, I thought someone was following me, and I got scared. I thought whoever killed Roland was probably after me. I just disappeared for several days. I deadened my phone, didn't open my mail, and did nothing but live in fear in my basement."

"I'm very sorry, Bernie. I'm fairly sure nobody was following you, at least nobody related to this case."

"I sent a couple of friends I could trust over to the church to give you the photo and message."

"They delivered your message, thank you. Do you feel okay now?" Belle asked.

"Yes. I'm all right. I'm just embarrassed for being so scared. I wanted to be brave, but all I did was put my head in the sand and hope the problem would go away."

"It is going away, Bernie. I think it'll all be explained soon. If you ever need help or a place to be, just come over here. Hank and I would be happy to keep you company."

"Thank you, Belle. You're a special lady."

"That's very sweet of you to say."

"Do you need any more from me?"

"I'm hoping to visit Lou Searing over in Grand Haven. Would you like to go with me? We'll put everything we have on the table and see if a pattern or two surfaces."

"Sure. I'm game."

♫ ♪ ♫ ♪ ♫

Since Belle had never been to see Lou, she fed his address into her GPS. She found herself south of Grand Haven on the old Holland Road, and soon, she saw "Searings!" on a sign nailed to a tree.

She turned in and followed a long drive until she came upon a home built into the dunes. Lou came out to greet his guests, Carol behind him, and Samm following Carol. The Searings embraced Belle, shook hands with Bernie, and invited them both into the house.

"Oh, my. Look at that view!" Belle exclaimed, as she looked out the back window. She could see for miles and miles out into Lake Michigan.

"My writing studio upstairs has the same magnificent view," Lou remarked.

Carol added with a smile, "And, my quilting studio is right next to Lou's office."

Millie, their cat, sauntered into the living room, wondering who had just invaded her territory. Belle and Bernie petted her to gain their acceptance in the house.

"Let me show you the rest of the house," Carol said.

While Belle and Bernie enjoyed the short tour, Lou checked his fax, e-mail, and phone for messages. He insisted he was not addicted to these devices, but he would have a hard time convincing anyone that they didn't control him somewhat.

Lou cleared off the dining room table so the three could work. He brought in a big bowl of potato chips, a bowl of dip, napkins, and a variety of soft drinks.

Carol excused herself, saying she had errands in town.

"Thank you for showing us your lovely home, Carol," Belle said. "This should be featured in one of those Home and Garden magazines. It's gorgeous."

"Thank you, Belle. Have a good meeting. I bet I'll come back to a solved mystery."

♫ ♪ ♫ ♪ ♫

One at a time, Belle, Lou, and Bernie shared their suspects, theories, evidence. When they had exhausted all possibilities, each was ready to offer a synopsis of what they thought had happened. Lou asked Bernie to go first.

"I do think Roland was murdered—by Drs. Handley and Waters. You'll never convince me that they did not kill Blake, too, and in time, might have killed me."

"Interesting," Lou said. "Thanks, Bernie. Now what about you, Belle?"

"Like Bernie," Belle began, "I believe Roland's death was a murder. I know this is a long shot but I think we should give credence to Reverend Norris as Roland's killer. He didn't like Roland. When Roland didn't show for the benefit Reverend Norris sponsored, the Reverend was furious. He had never been so embarrassed, and I think he needed revenge. He knew where Roland would be, and he knew of his allergy problem. He was confident no one would suspect him, being a preacher."

"Also interesting. Now I'll put forth my theory."

"What does the detective extraordinaire think?" Belle asked.

"I know this isn't fair after I asked you two for your theories, but I can't state with any assurance that A or B killed Roland, although like you two, I believe he was murdered.

"Handley and Waters probably didn't kill Roland, because the choir loft was unfamiliar to them, and I don't think they could know Roland's routine. Also, there's nothing we could present as evidence."

"Meaning?" Belle asked.

"Meaning no one saw either of them, no fingerprints, no clear proof either were involved."

"You are probably going to say the killer is someone at this table," Bernie said.

"Actually, Bernie, I did think of you because you knew Roland well enough to know of his allergy. But, I dismissed you for lack of a motive. He had been good to you in the Big Brother program."

"Mr. Searing, I swear I had nothing to do with his death," Bernie said earnestly.

"I'm with Lou," Belle replied. "Bernie is not our man." Bernie took a deep breath and settled back in his chair, relieved.

Lou continued, "I must be honest and tell you that I did seriously considered Winston, for the reasons we put on the table. But I believe his character is such that he simply could not kill anyone. Perhaps he could be involved if he was hired to kill Roland, but as I said, he just couldn't kill."

"He's a very sweet man," Belle said. "I know sometimes the sweet little old lady who wouldn't swat a fly turns out to be an axe-wielding witch, but Winston didn't do it. I agree with you there, Lou."

"Not only did you, Bernie, make it to my list, but so did you, Belle," Lou said, looking Belle in the eye.

"You've got to be kidding!" Belle responded, her mouth open in disbelief. "You really had me on your list?"

"Yes, for all the same reasons people in the church and the community thought maybe you were the killer. You were last to see Roland, your fingerprints were at the scene, and you knew of his allergy. But, as with Bernie, I really couldn't come up with a motive."

"Thank you, Lou Searing. I feel I've been pardoned by the governor while I sit on death row."

"I never had you seriously as a suspect, but you *might* have been the murderer."

Lou finally made a definitive statement, "The murderer is not someone in the choir."

"I agree, Belle said with conviction. "I know each member and like Bernie, me, and the janitor, there is simply no motive. Plus the choir are like family. It's totally out of the question,"

"Which brings us back to the question of who did have a motive," Lou said. "The one person left is Megan Morgan, at the group home."

"I thought of her, too, but rejected her as a suspect because I couldn't imagine her angry to the point of killing," Belle stated. "However, if the DNA results say that strand of hair belongs to Megan, she has to be our prime suspect. Agree?" Lou and Bernie nodded in unison.

"Now, if not Megan, I'd go with suicide," Lou continued.

"You really think he killed himself?" Belle asked.

"Of course we can't know what goes on in another's mind, but it could have been an easy escape from an unhappy life," Lou reasoned.

"I'm quite surprised that you aren't concluding a conspiracy between Dr. Handley and Ted Waters," Belle led.

"Well, as I said, I have neither of them on my list of prime suspects. Now having said all of this, I expect Megan Morgan to be the killer," Lou said, suddenly going from uncertainty to pointing a finger.

"So nobody has Phyllis as a suspect. How did she get out from under the radar?" Bernie asked.

"She did have peanuts with her in the choir loft and she didn't like Roland," Belle added.

"Yes. But, she has no motive," Lou said. "To be perfectly honest, it is more likely Roland killed himself so Phyllis would be a prime suspect."

"Interesting," Bernie said.

Belle added, "Lou, Waters has everything to gain with Roland dead. Why aren't you seeing him as the killer?"

"Waters is nothing but a scared, bumbling, liar, as evidenced throughout this case. He didn't kill anyone."

"Well, we've got more work to do, because someone out there did this. Or again, I keep coming back to a natural death. Why can't we accept this?" Belle said.

"Because of the peanut shells. Unless he wanted to commit suicide, Roland didn't put them there," Lou concluded. "I did some research and learned that there are several varieties of peanuts. To my knowledge, we haven't compared the shells on the floor with the peanuts in Phyllis's purse."

"Why does that seem so elementary?" Belle asked.

"In retrospect, it should have been the first thing you did in this investigation," Lou said, with a hint of criticism in his voice.

"Why didn't you suggest it to me, Lou?"

"I'm a proponent of learning by experience. I didn't see any harm in withholding that suggestion."

"Again, lesson learned," Belle said, shaking her head.

"Lou, I don't understand why Drs. Handley and Waters are not prime suspects. If they get the rights to the patent, they're eventually millionaires. Why can't we wrap our heads around the professor causing the lab explosion at the University of Wisconsin and then killing Roland? That would be the perfect place, because everyone would point to someone in the Living Waters Church," Bernie said, making a case for outsiders.

"Belle, can you answer his question?"

Without thinking, Belle exclaimed, "The facts just don't support that theory."

Lou pumped his fist in the air. "Wonderful answer, detective. You're learning. I'm proud of you!"

Belle smiled. "Thanks. Well, this has been an enlightening discussion, but I need to get home and we have a good three-hour drive ahead of us."

"We accomplished good work today," Lou said. "Thank you for coming over."

"Thank you, Lou. You and Carol have a beautiful home, and two affectionate pets. And, the views from your studios and living area are indescribable."

"For sure," Bernie added.

♫ ♪ ♫ ♪ ♫

Belle and Bernie had just backed out of the driveway when Lou's cell phone rang. He saw that it was Chief Purdy.

"Lou, I learned something that you and or Belle might find of interest."

"Belle just left. She has been here for the past two hours for a brainstorming session on the case. We didn't come to any conclusions, but the time was well spent."

"That's good to hear. I got a call from Mr. Handley."

"The professor's husband?"

"Yes. He found something I needed to know about."

"Peanuts, right?"

"How did you know?"

"I guess we're on the same frequency."

"He said it was out of character for his wife because she didn't like peanuts. She wasn't allergic—just didn't like them. He said that there hadn't been any in the house for decades."

"Hmm, that is odd."

"That's not all," Chief Purdy continued. "He said he found ice cream in their basement freezer."

"What's odd about that?" Lou asked.

"Apparently they never eat ice cream."

"So we have strange peanuts and ice cream in the professor's home. Interesting."

"Add them to your evidence file, Lou."

"What kind of ice cream was it?" Lou asked.

"Chocolate chip cookie dough," Chief Purdy replied.

"The flavor that was laced with rat poisoning," Lou replied.

The two exchanged farewells. Lou couldn't keep this to himself. He called Belle on her cell. Bernie answered

"Belle is driving?" Lou asked.

"Yes. Is there a message, or should she call you later?" Bernie asked.

"Tell her I just got off the phone with Chief Purdy. The professor's husband found peanuts and ice cream in their home, and they don't eat either—never have them in the house."

"I'll tell her. She may call you, Lou."

"No need. That's everything from the Chief's call."

Bernie passed the information on to Belle, who nodded matter-of-factly.

♫ ♪ ♫ ♪ ♫

Belle wanted to talk to Phyllis again, so the two met for coffee at the Chelsea Grille. After pleasantries were exchanged, Belle, asked, "Phyllis, may I have one of your peanuts?"

"May you what?" Phyllis replied, her voice rising.

"You told me you always carry peanuts in your purse, so you must have some."

"I do, but why do you want one?" she asked, puzzled. Suddenly her calm demeanor became disgust. "Ah, you still think I killed Roland. What can I do to prove my innocence?"

"You can give me a peanut."

"OK, here. Shall I leave a good fingerprint on it for you?"

"Phyllis, please calm down," Belle urged. "I'm at the point where I think Roland's death is related to peanuts. I'm sorry, but you must accept that a woman in the choir who carries peanuts is suspect."

"I guess you're right."

"I want one of your peanuts because I've learned about varieties of peanuts, and maybe yours are a different variety than the ones found near Roland's body. If they are the same, I will note that, and as much as it upsets you, you'll remain in my suspect file."

"I think I'm in luck. The peanuts I have are from my last flight east. I doubt the peanuts beside Roland came from an airline service."

"You're right. Please give me the packet."

"Oh, all right—you can keep it. I have more at home."

Belle knew instantly that the peanuts were not the same. It seemed a given that Phyllis was innocent. But, although the two women managed to change topics and enjoy the rest of their coffee and conversation, Belle still found herself thinking, *I really should look in her purse, but I've pushed enough.*

♫ ♪ ♫ ♪ ♫

Roland had a financial planner, Joe Brooks, for one thing that Roland followed closely was his finances. As soon as Mr. Brooks learned of Roland's death, he began to study the details of his estate. Joe managed to have the paperwork in order so it wouldn't be necessary to probate the will to settle Roland's affairs.

Joe scheduled a meeting with Megan. When she arrived, she accepted a cup of coffee and relaxed on the lush leather couch in the reception area. She was not particularly savvy of finances and law, but she was curious to hear what Mr. Brooks had to say.

Presently Megan was escorted into Mr. Brooks' office and offered a seat across from Joe. Once settled, she began to sip the warm coffee.

"Megan, I asked to meet with you because I am executor for Mr. Spencer's estate."

"I don't know what that means," Megan admitted.

"It's my job to settle his estate, to handle any outstanding debts, and to distribute funds to those Roland designated when he was alive."

"I see. And you wanted to talk to me about this?"

"Yes. We have procedures to follow, but I wanted you to know that your group home is the beneficiary of Mr. Spencer's estate. Were you aware of that?"

"No. I'm not sure what that means, either," Megan replied.

"It means that once expenses are paid and fees subtracted from the money that was his when he died, the remainder will go to your group home."

"You mean Mr. Spencer's will gives our home money?" Megan asked, dumbfounded.

"Yes, and the amount is substantial. It looks like the bequest is around five hundred thousand dollars. You will also receive some tangible assets like 100 gold coins.

"Also, Aria will receive several thousand for her care, along with Roland's CDs. Apparently Aria enjoys listening to music!"

"I guess she does," Megan replied, still not quite grasping the reality that Mr. Spencer had left such a large sum for the group home.

"I have some papers for you to sign, if you would, please," Joe said opening a manila envelope.

"I don't know what to make of this," Megan said, setting down her cup. "I think I want to talk to a lawyer myself."

"You can do so if you wish. I'd be happy to meet with your attorney. In fact that's probably a good idea."

Megan considered further. "Why would Mr. Spencer leave us all that money?"

"We'll never know. I imagine he liked Dick, appreciated his care of Aria, and saw in the home a charity that could use some financial help."

"I hated him!" Megan replied.

"You did?" Joe responded, surprised.

"He didn't pay Dick for Aria's care—promised to pay him every week."

"Hmm, that doesn't sound like Roland," Joe replied.

"Well, it was. I was constantly yelling at him, threatening him, hating the ground he stood on," Megan said disgustedly.

"How ironic. All this hate, yet he gives the home thousands of dollars. Doesn't make a lot of sense, does it?" Joe said, puzzled by this turn of events. "I suggest you contact your lawyer, and the three of us can discuss this bequest. In the meantime I will continue working through the estate. Agreeable?"

"Yes. Thank you."

Megan rose from her leather chair, picked up her wrap, and walked from the office in a daze.

13

Belle's home phone rang.

"Belle, this is Marian Eastman, Tom's wife. Can I come see you? I have something that you should have."

"Certainly. Come on over. I'll put on a pot of coffee and hope that Hank hasn't eaten all the chocolate chip cookies I baked yesterday."

"Thanks, I'll be right over."

When Belle opened the front door fifteen minutes later, Mr. and Mrs. Eastman stood on her porch. "Oh, hello," Belle said. "Come on in."

"Thank you, Belle."

"Let's sit in the living room. I'll bring in a plate of cookies and coffee. Do you take sugar or cream? Or maybe you would prefer tea?"

"We're coffee people, and we both drink it straight out of the pot," Tom replied.

"Okay. Make yourself at home. Hank is off playing bridge."

While Belle was in the kitchen, Tom whispered to Marian. "Are you sure you want to tell Belle?"

"I've prayed and prayed, and the feeling I get is that I must tell Belle."

"That's fine. I just want you to be certain of what you're about to do."

"I'm sure."

Belle returned to the living room. "These cookies were made yesterday."

"I'm sure they will be delicious, Belle."

"Well, if they are a bit dry, drink some coffee, and they'll soften right up."

When they were all sipping and munching, Belle began. "You wanted to tell me something, Marian? I must admit, I'm curious. I'm glad you're here, but couldn't you just tell me over the phone?"

"Well, I have prayed about this, and the answer I got is to tell you in person."

"Fine. What is on your mind?"

"About a month ago Roland gave me this sealed envelope. He told me not to open it. But, if he died, I was to wait a couple of weeks and then give it to the Chelsea Police."

"Strange," Belle said, raising her eyebrows.

"I agree. I did what he asked—I went to see Chief Purdy. He told me to give it to you, since you and another detective were trying to determine whether he was murdered."

"That was nice of him, I guess."

"Anyway, here it is," Marian said, handing Belle a business-size envelope. Belle set it on the coffee table in front of her.

"Aren't you going to open it?" Tom asked.

"Not right now. I want my attorney present, and perhaps Lou Searing."

"Why?"

"It seems innocent enough, but caution counts here."

"Caution?" Marian asked, disappointed.

"Yes, first of all, this could be evidence in my investigation and I don't want to tear it open, possibly disturbing whatever is inside. Secondly, I want the police to be present to witness the opening and to advise me on any legal procedures."

"I was hoping you would open it. Tom and I are curious—and have been ever since Roland died. I was sure you would satisfy our curiosity, too."

"The way I look at it, another day won't make a difference," Belle pointed out.

"The envelope is yours now, so you can do whatever you wish," Marian agreed.

The three sat rather uncomfortably for several minutes, sharing small talk and occasionally glancing at the envelope.

When the last cookie had been eaten, Marian rose saying, "Thank you for having us, Belle. We'll be on our way now."

"Thank you for coming over," Belle said, leading the couple to the door.

"Will you tell us what's in the envelope?" Tom asked.

"I most certainly will. That is, if legal counsel allows me to."

"Goodbye, Belle," Tom replied, and the couple walked to their car.

♫ ♪ ♫ ♪ ♫

Belle called Lou and explained the mystery surrounding the envelope.

"Very good, Belle. You did exactly what you should have done. I'm proud of you."

"Thanks, but what do I do now?"

"I'll call Chief Purdy and ask that he allow you to open the envelope in his presence, or perhaps he'll want to open it himself. A police officer should be on hand to take a photo of the contents. And he or she may want to wear protective gloves—the contents might be toxic."

"Really? It's just a business envelope, Lou. It just feels like a letter is all."

"Caution is key, Belle. The contents could explode, or it could simply be a letter. If it is a letter, not only is the written word important, but there may be some fingerprints on the paper. One can't be too careful when opening something, even when it seems unassuming."

"Okay, but I shan't open an envelope ever again without remembering this conversation."

"Don't fret. Chief Purdy will know what to do."

♫ ♪ ♫ ♪ ♫

The next morning, Belle headed to the police station, the envelope tucked safely in her purse. The officer at the reception desk buzzed Belle into the row of offices, where she was greeted by Chief Purdy. "Lou said to give this to you, and you would know what to do."

"Yes, I talked with him. Let's go back to the forensic room and see what we have. I want you to open it, but first put on these gloves and goggles."

"Is this really necessary?" Belle asked, shaking her head.

"How's that saying go, 'Better safe than sorry'?"

"I know." She struggled into the gloves. "Do I just open it like any letter?"

"Use this letter-opener, and carefully slit the envelope across the top."

"Wait a minute. Why am I doing this? You open it Chief, or have one of your officers open it!"

"Oh, don't be ridiculous."

"Ridiculous? You dress me like I'm diffusing a bomb and then you run. You remind me of my dental hygienist who throws a hundred pounds of lead over my body and runs for cover, claiming the x-ray test is safe. Right!"

Chief Purdy chuckled. "All will be well, Belle. We're taking common-sense precautions. Go ahead and open it. I'm sorry to make a big deal out of this. Normally I'd just have you open it, but Mr. Searing seemed adamant about using caution. I respect him, so I'm cautious."

Belle slowly opened the envelope; inside was a one-page, typed letter. To find only a letter was disappointing in a way, but everyone was relieved the contents were not laced with anthrax or something else dangerous. The letter read,

> *To Whom It May Concern:*
>
> *If you are reading this, I assume I am dead. If my death has been explained to the satisfaction of the authorities this can be destroyed. But, if people are still wondering what happened, this letter may be helpful.*
>
> *The authorities may have searched my past and discovered my relationship with a U of M professor, Dr. Marcia Handley and two graduate school colleagues, Blake Schooley and Ted Waters. Ted Waters believes Professor Handley arranged for Blake's death. I do not believe this. I think it*

was an accident. Ted will undoubtedly point to Professor Handley as playing a part in my death. I don't think this would be the case. Of any one of the three in my chemistry background, I would bet Ted would play a part in my demise, for he would have the most to gain if I were out of the picture.

As far as other possibilities, Phyllis will be a prime suspect because she carries peanuts and doesn't like me. But, Phyllis has a pure soul, and while we were not close friends, I can't believe that she would risk life in prison to shorten my life.

Reverend Norris should be off the suspect list.

Dick Fox cared for my dog, Aria. He would not participate in a murder. Granted, I didn't pay him properly, but he loved Aria and simply put up with me. I appreciated Dick's work and was glad he could live in the group home in our community. I have made up not paying him regularly by leaving my estate to the group home.

Someone might suggest I committed suicide, but nothing would be further from the truth. I plan to live my life until my God calls me home. Do not believe anyone who suggests I took my own life.

Yes, I'm allergic to peanuts, and like people with bee stings, I could very well die if I encountered them and found no help. I took a risk this week by not filling my prescription for relief of anaphylaxis symptoms.

So, IF I was murdered, who do I think was my killer? Belle Franklin is at the top of my list. I firmly believe that her vision of the perfect choir had no deep bass. She knew she could never convince me to leave. I believe she couldn't wait for my natural death and therefore hurried mine along.

For what it is worth, it really matters not who, if anyone, killed my physical life. I had a good life and am in a better place now.

Roland Spencer

The police chief made a copy of the letter and kept the original in the evidence file.

Belle left the station puzzled. She held Roland's letter in her hand. She wasn't happy about being named Roland's murderer, especially after spending considerable time trying to solve the puzzle. But, Belle recognized that Roland was simply offering his opinion, even though he was wrong.

♫ ♪ ♫ ♪ ♫

Belle read and reread the letter, trying to understand Roland's thinking. She called Lou to share the contents.

"Interesting. I've not heard of a victim leaving a letter giving his or her perceptions of a possible murderer. But, we need to focus on other things. Like where did the peanuts come from? Who poisoned the ice cream? Why did that professor take her life? Why did Ted feel a need to leave town? It's like you found a major piece for your puzzle, but now you need to find the remaining pieces to complete the picture so that it makes sense. Do you follow?"

"Yes, I understand what you are saying."

"Unless you can account for all the facts around a case, you're not likely to convince the police, the populace, or a judge and jury that your scenario is valid."

♫ ♪ ♫ ♪ ♫

Belle received a call from Chief Purdy. "We made a huge mistake, Belle. I just visited Reverend Norris and apologized profusely."

"Goodness! What did you do, anyway?"

"When we returned the ice cream to the church freezer, we brought the wrong container. We had the one that contained rodent poisoning pellets embedded in the ice cream. A student had laced the container. Anyway, we thought we were bringing the right container and well, you know the rest of the story."

"Oh my, thank goodness Reverend Norris is alive."

"I almost break into a sweat thinking of his dying because of our error."

"Well, one good fact to come out of this is that ice cream was not a factor in Roland's death."

"Yes. One of my detectives reexamined the receipts from the grocery purchases the night Roland died, and you were right—the man in front of you bought the ice cream."

"As I said."

"I know, forgive me for doubting you—it won't happen again. Your credibility is good with me."

♫ ♪ ♫ ♪ ♫

Tim Traxler saw Belle at the mall and approached her. "Have you solved the Roland mystery?"

"We're making progress, but we're not ready to declare it solved," Belle replied.

"Did the people who played CLUE at our booth give you an idea?"

"What do you mean?"

"Reverend Norris told us to stop our marketing game at the craft show and return the guesses people made about Roland's death to him. We did so, and I'm wondering if he or you got any insights?"

"I never heard about this," Belle replied.

"Ask Reverend Norris. He may have thrown them away."

"I will. Glad you mentioned this to me."

Belle called Reverend Norris, who was recuperating at home, and asked about the CLUE entries.

"Oh yes. Those are in the side drawer of my desk with a rubber band around them."

"Did you find anything interesting?" Belle asked.

"I never even read them. They were meaningless to my way of thinking."

"Have I permission to retrieve them from your desk?"

"Of course."

Belle went right to his desk and took out the small bundle of guesses. She quickly read through them, finding nothing of real interest until she saw, "Phyllis did it with peanuts in the choir loft."

The entrant's name and address was: Megan Morgan, Arthur Hills Group Home.

Belle put the entries back into the Reverend's desk and drove over to see Megan. They sat alone in the common room.

"Were you at the craft show last week?" Belle asked.

"Oh, yes. Best show in the area. I go every year."

"Did you stop at the Traxler booth and write down a guess as to how Roland died?"

"I enter every contest I can. I liked the prize, a fashionable purse, so I entered."

"Reverend Norris had taken all of the entries and yours says, 'Phyllis did it with peanuts in the choir loft.'"

Megan let out a hearty laugh. "Good guess, huh? Are you here to tell me I won?"

"No, I'm hoping you can explain your guess," answered Belle seriously.

"While I was at the booth, thinking of an answer, I asked a man next to me if he had any suggestions. He didn't hesitate. "'Phyllis killed him with peanuts.'"

"Who was the man?" Belle asked.

"I have no idea."

"Do you remember what he looked like? Did he have any identifying features?"

"You know, I didn't even make eye contact with him. I just said, 'thanks' and he drifted away. I wrote down what he had said, adding 'in the choir loft' because the newspaper said that was where he died."

"Who knows, you may have the answer. But you do know that there will be no prize. This death is serious business, not a childish game."

"I understand and I agree."

"Thanks for talking with me," Belle said, rising and turning toward the door.

"Certainly. And while you are here, thanks again for giving Aria to Dick. They are wonderful companions."

"I'm glad that story has a happy ending," Belle remarked.

14

Samples of DNA were taken from everyone considered a suspect. The results of the DNA test came to Lou in a timely manner, with the indication that the strand of hair belonged to Phyllis. Lou called Belle. "How is that for a surprise?"

"I never thought she was a killer."

"There you go again, jumping to conclusions. All we know is that the hair belongs to Phyllis," Lou cautioned. "It doesn't mean she killed Roland."

"Maybe not, but it's fairly convincing."

"True, but the hair could have been planted there by the killer. Or, she was in Roland's spot distributing music. Or the vacuum, if one was used, could have left the strand there when the machine was turned off."

"Or, someone could have found the strand on Phyllis's robe before choir practice, and planted it on the floor with broken peanuts," Belle added.

"Yes, that could have happened. Or, the killer simply needed a strand of hair and randomly found a strand on Phyllis's robe. It didn't matter whose hair it was. It would take attention off the killer and put it on the unsuspecting choir member."

"I'm amazed by how complex this can be," Belle admitted.

"Right. When you work the crime-solving puzzle, not only does each piece of the puzzle have to fit, but also the whole puzzle must be complete and the entire story must be told."

"I have it now, Lou. This opens up a lot of possibilities."

"Definitely. The killer could be Phyllis, Reverend Norris, the janitor, even sweet Mrs. Sneath."

"I really thought we were getting close to solving this," Belle said dejectedly.

"We are. And again, Roland could have dropped the strand there along with peanuts if he was in fact suicidal."

"I need a cup of coffee. It seems I'm back to square one."

"Take a break from it, Belle. Get your mind on something else and come back to it refreshed."

Since the evidence pointed directly at Phyllis, Belle felt a need to confront her. Instead of calling, she went to her home.

Phyllis answered the door with a sigh. "As much as I enjoy your company, Belle, I think this is more about my peanuts. Am I right?" They took chairs in the living room.

"I'm sorry, but the evidence points to you, Phyllis. I don't want to believe it, but either you are the killer, or someone is making you out to be."

"It's got to be the latter, Belle. What have you heard, if I may ask?"

"A strand of hair was found along with the peanuts near Roland's body. DNA results show it belongs to you. You recall the CLUE contest at the craft show?"

"Yes."

"One of the entries read, 'Phyllis did it with a peanut in the choir loft.' Everyone knows that you carry peanuts in your purse, and that you did not like Roland. The strand of hair is most damning at this point."

"I don't know what to say, Belle. I would swear on a stack of Bibles—I'm innocent."

"Then, somebody is framing you. Who might want to do this, Phyllis?"

"I didn't think I had any enemies."

"And, maybe you don't. There are logical reasons for your hair being in Roland's area of the loft. For example, someone including Roland, could have lifted a strand of your hair off of your choir robe and placed it in the loft. Let's assume it was not Roland, if someone did take it from your robe. Who else would want you as the prime suspect?"

"I honestly don't know, Belle."

"Tell me about your choir robe. And, go back a few weeks."

"My robe?" Phyllis asked, sounding confused.

"Yes, did it ever leave the choir room? Did you take it home for some reason?"

"I'm sure it went to the cleaners a couple of weeks ago."

"Just a cleaning?" Belle asked.

"Now that I think about it, the hem was coming apart, and I guess the cleaner sewed it up. The tailor did a nice job because the hem was perfect the next time I put it on."

"Anything else?"

"I don't think so."

"Have you ever seen this woman?" Belle produced a photo of Megan.

"She came to the choir loft at one of our practices. She said she had a message for Roland, remember?"

"Yes, I do," Belle replied. "I asked if it was private or if she could tell him from a distance."

"That's right," Phyllis recalled. "She said Dick would not be able to care for his dog for a few days."

"Yes. And, Roland replied, 'Okay, I'll take care of it' or words to that effect."

"That's my recollection."

Suddenly Belle rose. "I have an idea I need to follow up on. Thanks for talking to me, Phyllis."

♫ ♪ ♫ ♪ ♫

Belle knew that the church patronized Chelsea Cleaners for their uniforms, robes and other cleaning and pressing jobs. She drove to the cleaners, walked in and spoke to the owner, Darlene Wang.

"If you need to repair a garment brought in for cleaning, do you do the repair, or do you send it out to a tailor?"

"We contract with a woman to do it."

"May I ask her name?"

"We have the name in our records. I do know she runs a group home for men with disabilities."

"Do you recall asking her to repair the hem in a choir robe?"

"Yes, she did a few hems as I recall."

Just as the evidence had seemed to point to Phyllis, now it seemed to point to Megan. Belle tallied some information quickly. She wrote in her notepad: *Very angry with Roland; knows where he sat in the loft; could have lifted a strand off of Phyllis's robe; had peanuts resembling those near Roland's body.* And Megan had made the prediction on the CLUE entry that Phyllis killed Roland. Megan was as much of a suspect as Phyllis, if not more.

Belle called Mr. Handley to ask about the strange peanuts and ice cream in their home. "Oh, thanks for calling. I think I can explain why we had ice cream and peanuts. My wife got the ice cream for an upcoming birthday party for a neighbor. And our son purchased the peanuts because he had read a book on healthy eating habits. Eating so many peanuts a day is supposedly good for one's health."

Belle was relieved. "Okay. It looks like the peanut-ice cream involvement in my case is not related to your wife or family."

"Apparently not."

"Good, I'm glad to be able to explain and close this aspect of the investigation."

♫ ♪ ♫ ♪ ♫

Belle finished her analysis of Ted Waters' involvement, reasoning that his behavior was the result of acute anxiety. He was certain that he would be thought guilty of Blake's death and of Roland's apparent murder. Wisconsin State Police considered him as their lead suspect in Blake's death, and they had questioned him extensively because of the ongoing challenge to the patent. The end result of their investigation was that Blake's death was an accident. Roland had also been a suspect, but when he died, it simply increased the likelihood that Ted was involved. When Ted confided in Marcia she tried to convince him that he would not be suspect, but her words fell on deaf ears.

Ted admitted that Belle had accurately described his state of mind. He was relieved that Belle was convinced he had nothing to do with either Blake's or Roland's death.

Belle called Lou, who answered on the second ring. "Yes, Belle. Good news?"

"Yes, I think so. I'm ready to tie up this investigation. Neither Ted nor Marcia Handley played a part in Roland's death. I am sure that Phyllis is guilt-free. Neither Winston, nor Reverend Norris had anything to do with it. I've played all the cards, Lou. I am certain that Megan Morgan is the murderer."

"The jackpot's yours, Belle."

"I assume I now contact Chief Purdy to sum up my findings and send this case to the courts."

"Amen, Belle. Amen."

EPILOGUE

Belle Franklin was relieved to finally have Roland's death explained. Her first investigation was a success.

Megan Morgan was charged with the murder of Roland Spencer. She was tried, found guilty, and sentenced to life in a women's correctional facility. At the trial, Megan admitted that her anger had escalated to rage against Roland. She admitted to placing a strand of hair she found on the choir robe she was mending for the Chelsea Dry Cleaners. She had played the role perfectly while meeting with Joe Brooks, for she had heard a month before from Mr. Hills, the president of the parent company that Mr. Spencer had designated the group home as his estate beneficiary. She couldn't wait for a natural death to receive the money. She plotted to make it look as if Phyllis had killed Roland.

A new supervisor was hired, and life at the group home returned to normal. The first installment of Roland's bequest was used to totally renovate the home.

Lou Searing was proud of his protégé and predicted that she would work on many more cases.

Dr. Ted Waters remains a chemist at Dow Chemical Company in Midland, Michigan.

The suicide of **Dr. Marcia Handley** was explained by the trouble she was in and the likely consequences once the truth was revealed.

Reverend Norris returned to excellent health. But, to this day, refuses to have even one bite of ice cream—no matter the flavor or the occasion.

Phyllis no longer carries peanuts in her purse.

Dick Fox and **Aria** are lifelong buddies. Roland's estate now promptly pays for Aria's care.

Winston Saturn returned to Holy Living Waters Church but refuses to set foot in the choir loft.

Bernie Higgins slipped away into obscurity.

Mrs. Sneath retired mid-summer. She wanted to be free of all the curious visitors stopping at the church wanting to see where Roland died.

The Peanuts found in Phyllis's purse, at the group home, and around Roland's body were the same variety. Belle never divulged this information to anyone, realizing this evidence didn't clearly point to one suspect.

The patent for CURB Lawn Spray remains tied up in the courts. Ted doesn't expect the matter to be resolved in his lifetime.

The Easter presentation of The Messiah was performed in the high school auditorium before a packed house. The tribute to Roland was a fitting remembrance of a talented virtuoso.

Oh, why Chelsea, Michigan? **Karen Bumstead** asked me to set one of my books in Chelsea—so a promise fulfilled.

THE END

A TRIBUTE

The Conversation Before Breakfast

Norah Hoffmeister, our four-year-old, eighth grandchild —and the second Queen in the Baldwin line of royalty—is a true princess. From dress, to accessories, to hats, to shoes, Norah lives part-time in a fantasy world. Her family, as well as Carol and I, enjoy watching this princess define her own world around the mirror presented to her.

Last summer the Hoffmeister family visited. For most of the day there were activities, meals, excursions to craft shows, visits to MSU venues (Michigan 4-H Garden, Red Cedar River, Museum). Norah, being the youngest, couldn't get a word in edgewise, but it didn't seem to matter, since she was living in her own world anyway.

One morning an early-to-rise Grandpa and an equally early-bird Norah found ourselves in the kitchen—just the two of us. As I made breakfast, Norah took the stage and, before I could put Cheerios in a bowl, was chattering about this, that, and the other. In spite of my hearing loss, I listened intently, determined not to miss a word.

What bliss, to have one-on-one time with a princess. Everyone else slept on while the two of us conversed about our lives. Today, I can't recall a single question or comment, but it was not what was said, but what was going on that I treasure: Time alone with Norah, establishing a relationship, taking an interest in each other. That conversation before breakfast with Norah remains etched fondly in my memory.